A True Odyssey

From: Hector Sanguino
To: Roberto.
The Friends are More
important than Money

Hector Sanguino

A True Odyssey

Héctor Sanguino

www.librosenred.com

C.E.O.: Marcelo Perazolo
Cover Design: Stefanie Sancassano
Interior Design: Vanesa L. Rivera

Revision and correction by Tamara Schurch
Official English Translator Certificate.
tcschurc@ucalgary.ca

Design, typesetting, and other prepress work by LibrosEnRed
www.librosenred.com

ISBN: 978-1-59754-974-5

First English Edition - Print on Demand

LibrosEnRed©
A trade mark of Amertown International S.A.
editorial@librosenred.com

TABLE OF CONTENTS

*Those who easily lose courage will
never know the pleasure of victory*

Hector J Sanguino Jr

To the memory of my grandparents,
Roberto Ortiz and Telmira Álvarez.
May God cover them with his cloak

Special gratitude to

Tamara Schurch, Leslye A Sanguino and all my teachers for their valuable collaboration in this literary work.

Prologue

This is a story about Moisés Fernandez, a humble man who was obligated since childhood to confront his destiny in order to survive. Although his life dealt him much adversity, his misfortunes never defeated him. Even when he found no light, his warrior spirit would challenge and triumph over adversity.

His misfortunes hurt the people whom Moisés loved most, and this was more painful than if he had been harmed directly. His battle against destiny led him to experience a series of incredible events, which were accompanied by short times of happiness and long periods of bitterness and sadness.

Achieving his goals wasn't easy, but Moisés's courage and persistence enabled him to accomplish what seemed impossible. However, shortly after each triumph, his life would fall back into misfortune; even so, he continued in his battle. In the middle of his struggle he would meet Mayra, his first love and a woman who loved him deeply. However, her parents, who sought an economic future for her, separated the couple against their will. Although destiny placed several obstacles in the couple's path, they maintained hoped to reunite one day. But nine years later, Moisés and Mayra would lose hope of meeting again. Their love would be suspended by time, waiting to be revived.

In his adulthood, Moisés concluded from the wisdom of his experiences, that he could change his own destiny and those of others by helping them. One of these individuals would be Hansel, who would eventually become a successful man.

Hansel's Conclusion

On the evening of the company's anniversary, one of the shareholders was recounting his life-story in front of the audience. "I was twelve when my mother died" he began. "Due to this calamity, my stepfather, who had a debt to pay after losing a bet, decided to sell me as merchandise to the Chinese mafia. In China they forced me into slavery. I worked long hours in an electronics factory without pay," he continued. "One night four years later, exhausted and distraught from working as a slave and from my unhealthy diet, I became desperate to escape. That night I stole away, but one of the night guard's saw me and attacked me. I lost an eye, but managed to escape and recover my freedom. I was frightened and running away from the Chinese mafia, who were closing in on me. I searched relentlessly for refuge and found hiding by the port in an old warehouse. Days later, I became a stowaway on a mercantile ship. During the sea crossing, I was discovered and the crew forced me into hard labour again for weeks. Three months later, when the ship finally made its first stop, the captain ordered the crew to leave me at the seaport. Without money and unable to speak a word of Spanish, my arrival to this new country would mark the beginning of a true odyssey. For several days I walked aimlessly, starving and alone. One evening, while I slept on a piece of cardboard that I used as a mattress in a back alley, someone picked me up and gave me shelter. This family's generosity and kindness enabled me to get back onto my feet.

They taught me Spanish and gave me a job as an assistant to an electrician, a skill I had already learned. I already knew about all of the cheapest electronics bought wholesale in China, but the most important thing was that I could communicate with people and bargain for the best price in their own language. This advantage would open doors to me in the business world and with my employer we would eventually start a small import company." With these words pride spread across his face. "Five years later," he continued beaming, "I became independent and created my own appliance factory. I made a deal with the Sanyo Corporation, what was considered then to be the greatest company in the world and patented my brand 'Sango.' This proved to be a successful business venture and soon my products were being displayed and sold throughout Latin America. The business grew quickly and it soon became a multinational corporation." A few seconds before ending his speech, he recognized how ironic it was that his experience as a slave worker had been the best thing that had ever happened to him. It was, he said, the ironic first step to becoming a successful man.

This amazing story astounded ninety nine percent of his audience. In fact, I was the only one who was not in the least bit impressed by the shareholder's life-story. I knew that Moisés, my friend and member of the Board of Directors who would be presenting to the same audience a little later, had experienced not only one, but many similar episodes. Of course, in order to show respect, I paid attention to this man's odyssey. However, I was aware that the shareholder's story was receiving attention, not because of the tragedy he had experienced but rather because the members of the audience had lived lives completely removed from such trauma and these experiences seemed impossible to them. When they did not see any expression of amazement in my face, they wanted to know the cause of my indifference. "Why aren't you surprised by this story?" they demanded. "The shareholder's experiences are insignificant in comparison to Moisés's odyssey, who I consider a true life warrior", I answered. "Although without doubt, the shareholder seems like a hero, he is a hero of few battles", I added. My answer produced even more confusion. They were curious and wanted to know more. "Why do you consider Moisés a true life warrior?" they asked. "It's a little ironic", I said "because he was a man who challenged his own destiny and managed to beat it". They became intrigued by my answers, and were eager to hear more. They wanted to know what Moisés did to become a true life warrior. I would proudly relate the story in great detail, revealing Moisés's challenges and the outcome of his epic life. With great pride I began to tell them my own story. The remarkable story of how I met Moisés. I returned in my mind's eye to a desperate and emotional time in my life.

"It was a winter morning in January of 2005", I began. "I was alone on a hill after having grappled with my problems for days. My crises had left me feeling desperate and trapped, as if in tight web. Some of my ideas were good and others bad. But after reflecting on each of the possible solutions in my mind, I reached the conclusion that putting a bullet through my head would be the only way to end my grief. For that reason, on that fateful winter morning I found myself shirtless on a hill side with a revolver in my right hand. I had placed two explosive 38 caliber long bullets in its chamber a few minutes earlier. Within moments, I began practicing a very dangerous game with the gun, known by many as "Russian roulette."

My first suicide attempt was not successful. So I took the revolver again, and while pointing the barrel toward the ground, gave the chambers a sharp twist in order to make my second attempt.

While l was contemplating this terrible idea, a cold breeze suddenly swept up the small hill, penetrating my body and chilling my bones. But the sudden frigid air failed to impact me because l was like a zombie, a body without a soul. Little did I know, that at that very moment I was not as alone as I believed; someone from the other side of the hill was watching me intently. He approached me silently like a feline pursuing its prey. His steps were so soft that a dry leaf falling would make more noise than his movements. My mind was so focused on putting an end to my existence that I did not notice the man at first. But my desperate plan to commit suicide would be interrupted by the man's sudden appearance. I would soon learn of his intention to sabotage my next attempt. Conscious and worried about my impulsive decision, he was afraid not to make it in time to save me. From far away he had seen desperation written on my face that had foretold a tragic ending.

This man was an angel sent from heaven with a mission to save my life and change my attitude. Although, his intervention was meant to save my life, at that moment in time it conflicted with my intentions. The man arrived at the precise moment that I was going to pull the trigger of the gun for the second time. He placed his right hand on my shoulder, and with the other pushed my arm, managing to divert the bullet's trajectory. I was shocked and stunned by the noise of my own gun. "What happened?" I exclaimed. Feeling his hand on my shoulder, he made me understand that I was not alone. In the midst of my confusion, I turned around and pointed the revolver at the intruder, angry that he had disturbed my suicide attempt. My first thought was to pull the trigger and shoot him, but in his eyes I perceived an infinite goodness and trust that forced me to abort my attack.

The strange character didn't pronounce a single word nor make any movement, but the strength of his gaze held my attention. When I finally managed to divert his gaze, the man said in a self-assured and calm voice, "Joven! No matter how difficult your problems are, there is always a solution".

Intrigued by his words, he managed to momentarily shake me out of my zombie state. He put his hand next to mine, and slowly took the gun from my hands. After his act of bravery he said confidently: "Please, tell me your story. I hope that I can help you". Although at that moment I did not believe in anybody, this man inspired enough trust in me that I began to unburden my heart to him. I began to tell him my story in great detail and divulge all my problems, both past and present. These problems continued to weigh heavily on my soul, and were the cause of profound pain. In a span of several hours I began to feel a sense of relief, but at the same time it confused me because I didn't understand why I had just vented my problems to a complete stranger.

This stranger was Moisés.

After listening to his advice and analyzing the possible solutions that he gave me for each of my dilemmas, I could feel myself slowly breaking out of my lethargic state. When he noticed my new attitude, he optimistically professed that he could solve my problems. However, I remained stubborn in my decision to kill myself, and didn't believe him. "Life has no meaning for me", I told him slightly irritated. "Everything I do turns out badly and become a frustration; each business venture has led me into debt, to the point where I'm completely broke. I don't have any self-confidence anymore and all of this has had disastrous effects on my family. What I've experienced hasn't given me wisdom but forced me to make terrible decisions. My mistakes, like an infinite line of falling dominos, have driven me to such utter madness that I've come to the conclusion that my only way out is to end my miserable existence with a single-shot. Had you not interrupted me, I would have solved all of my problems with a bullet to my head" I said to him. At that moment, I didn't see Moisés as my savior. On the contrary, I felt that he was at fault for my continued existence. Moisés was looking at me carefully, noticing the displeasure in my eyes. Worried by my negative attitude, he placed his hands squarely on my shoulders. "I understand your situation," he said. "But the only non-viable solution to your problems is death and nobody should reach that extreme no matter how difficult their circumstances are. You have to act wisely and exhaust all of your options" he told me firmly. "What is happening to you is not that complicated. If you look carefully, you can change your life. Your biggest mistake is trying to solve all your problems at once, and this is very difficult if not impossible. Remember that everything in life contains a process. So, solve your dilemmas one by one. When you have solved the first problem then go on to the next. You are not trapped in a maze with no exit. If you have financial difficulties, face the people you owe and explain your situation to them. I am sure that they will understand and give you time to pay them back. Although your debts won't go away because of your agreement, some more time will allow you to relax and think calmly while looking for an alternative solution. If your first attempt does not produce the expected result, try a second option". His wise words reminded me of how young people always look for excuses to their problems and many never explore more than three possible options when trying to solve a problem or while pursuing a dream. "Now a days, he continued," young people give up without ever seeing their dreams come to fruition. Life teaches us that whoever is most persistent will eventually succeed and reach their goal." He reminded me of Thomas Edison, who in order to invent the light bulb, made more than four hundred attempts. To be the greatest inventor in history was not easy for him. He found many bumps along the road but they didn't present obstacles to him becoming a successful man. With his invention", Moisés contested, "he taught us two principals: his legacy and the courage to exhaust all possible options".

With these words, Moisés changed the fatalistic way I saw my life. I soon learned that he had also overcome many not only difficult, but devastating situations. He had experienced the excruciating torment of seeing attacks and harm come to those he loved most. More than once these events had left him so distraught and desperate, it was like being pushed onto the edge of a precipice.

When I compared my experiences to his, I understood that in fact I had only experienced small obstacles in my life. My suffering was inconsequential compared to what he had been through. My misfortune was mostly due to being in the wrong place or by making hasty decisions. The series of negative events had engulfed me in adversity, and instead of thinking things through calmly, I acted hastily, even rashly, leading to more misfortune and the point of wanting to end my life.

The philosophical words of Moisés, emanating through his rough and throaty voice at one point became overshadowed by the noise from an old oak tree. A strong breeze had caused the branches to crash against each other. But his fluid lexicon and perfect vocalization kept me fixated on his story. His smaller stature was inexplicably impacting. His balding head had progressed down to the nape of his neck, and made it seem like he had a shaved head. His Jeans, running shoes and a tight black T-shirt exhibited an athletic musculature that revealed his muscle fibers when he used his arms. Everything that was normal in Moisés produced admiration in me. His amazing adventures, his heroic story and the events that he had experienced had erased all thoughts of suicide from my mind. I was impressed by his military experience, the sufferings of his past, his metaphors and how his own strength of character had challenged his destiny. I became filled with new optimism and the desire to never give up nor succumb to life's woes. His experiences were so unusual they produced an emotional story, like no other I've ever heard.

THE STORY

Moisés was nostalgic for June 13th, 1963. On that evening, Juana, the village midwife, helped bring a baby into the world from Mariela Fernandez's abdomen, a baby she considered a miracle due to the difficult birth. Moisés told me that an electrical storm blew into town on the evening of his premature birth. One of the lightning bolts cut the electrical power for several minutes, and it was at that precise moment that he was born. During childbirth, in the darkness, his mother Mariela fell off the bed and dislocated her shoulder.

But Moisés's odyssey already had begun before his birth, when his mother found herself in the first weeks of pregnancy. The hemorrhage came suddenly. As a result of Mariela's continual bleeding, she was prone to miscarriage, a condition that could threaten her life. Furthermore, because of the economic crisis, she could not go to the hospital. She remained under the strict care of her midwife, and fortunately due to her care, managed to move forward with her pregnancy. These negative events made Moisés's mother turn to the Bible in order to find a name for her baby. She decided that her son would be called Moisés. He didn't know with certainty if the prophet's name had been just a coincidence, or if it was one of his mother's premonitions; a vision of the many challenges that would face her child during his life, a life that would also be lived with great courage. Before his birth, just as after, Moisés would face large periods of sadness interrupted by short moments of happiness, which would leave his soul confused; a soul that from an early age would begin to battle against adversity. But he would defy his own destiny day by day, overcoming his obstacles and ultimately winning his battles.

As a bastard son, he was discriminated against by his father's family, who since his birth rejected him. They saw the child as an impediment to his father's happiness since in those days an illegitimate child would cause problems when wishing to marry. Moisés's father's attitude filled Mariela with sadness, who as a result of being abandoned by him, cried all the time. She felt guilty for his behavior, but in reality she was innocent. She carried the seed of a bad man in her who had disguised himself as a meek lamb, professing his deep love and commitment to her so that she would give him what was considered to be her most valuable treasure: her virginity. After seducing Mariela, the cursed man left her with a lot to think about because only two weeks later, she became pregnant. Sadness clouded over Moisés's face as he continued telling me his story. He talked to me about his childhood and told me that he never received any help from his father, while his mother, who was suffering from sciatica from washing the neighbours' clothes in the river, struggled every day to provide for them.

However, along with these memories he recalled others of great joy. He remembered fondly of the times he spent with his uncle Antonio, his mother's brother. After having been separated for many years from his sister Mariela, Antonio, as if by magic, appeared in her life again. Although his arrival brought them joy and well-being, this would only be temporary. Many weeks after his arrival they would lose him forever. Moisés recalled ironically how his uncle used to tell him his favorite fable, "A beautiful dream". He would hear this story about tolerance every night while falling asleep on his uncle's chest. The reason why Moisés described this experience so ironically was because his uncle Antonio's humble appearance camouflaged an impulsive and violent nature. This nature would cause his early departure from this world and would plunge Moisés and his mother into a prolonged melancholic state.

When his uncle was at home, he always showed them love and respect. He was a brave man and an expert fighter, and the town's people soon learned that he wasn't afraid of anyone. However, his radical decisions would sometimes worry his sister Mariela and cause her great distress. The way he would tell people directly what he thought and openly criticize their behaviour, created many problems for him. On more than one occasion, he received to their attackers with a slap in the face for their offensive behaviour. He would especially go to great lengths in order to defend his family and friends when humiliated. He would act impulsively but with courage, unwilling to let anyone trample his loved ones. Despite his courage to do what he believed to be right, his uncle Antonio's radical behaviour would earn him several enemies and instigate many fights.

A day came when his enemies had had enough. They joined together and planned to kill him. His death would take place one warm afternoon in the market square. On that crucial Sunday the aggressors, armed with knives, axes and guns, attacked his uncle while he was in the butcher shop. Although alone, his uncle Antonio bravely faced his attackers and killed two of them, but he was powerless to defend himself against the rest. At that moment, Antonio's friends and Mariela, who were close by, could see the danger he was in and ran to his side in order to defend him. The fight that ensued would cause several deaths and injuries. During the massive attack on his uncle, his friends were massacred behind his back, and although Mariela's life was spared, she was shot in the leg twice with 22 caliber bullets.

Months after the attack, when Moisés was attending kindergarten, he had to confront more of life's harshness. He no longer had his uncle there to defend him when he was mocked by some of the children and become the butt of their jokes. They would make fun of him because Moisés's father didn't accompany him to school as theirs did. On many occasions, Moisés would walk to school alone because his mother was too busy working as a laundress, washing other family's clothing.

However, the way the children picked on Moisés greatly upset his teacher Teresa, and she would talk to the parents of the aggressors who then promised her that their children would be reprimanded. After her efforts a few of them stopped bothering Moisés, but others, who had never been scolded or punished, continued to make fun of him with even more rancor. They always found a way to offend Moisés. They would humiliate his mother by calling him "the laundress's son", a nick name that he wouldn't shed for many years and would haunt him into his adulthood.

Moisés spoke as if he were an open book with nothing to hide. He began to tell me about his adolescence, a more positive chapter in his life. At that time he could count on the unconditional support of Teresa, his teacher who for many years helped him with school supplies and uniforms. On Christmas day she would give him a beautiful new set of clothing. Her generous support however, would come to an end when he started fifth grade. Teresa got married and decided to settle down in another town with her new husband. Despite her physical absence in Moisés's life, she still kept in touch with him and tried to help him from a distance. Sometimes he received letters and books by famous writers from her. In one of the letters years later, his ex-benefactor would tell him that she now had to support the underprivileged children in her own school and could no longer help him. However, the fact that Teresa's generosity continued easing the lives of other unfortunate children filled Moisés with happiness. In the middle of this nostalgic memory, Moisés recognized that her teachings and the books she sent him had been an essential part of his education. It was largely due to her generosity and kindness that he was able to withstand much of the hardship destiny would place in his path.

In school, Moisés would also make a true friend with whom he shared everything. They were inseparable during recess, and after school they were often up to some kind of mischief. Joel Pérez, his friend, went to junior high school with him. A few years later, in high school they would again share the same classroom for a couple of years.

Moisés paused, sighed deeply, and then continued to tell his story.

He recounted the moment in high school, when his mother began to suffer from a strange disease. Because of her illness he had to give up school during the day and study at night. This would separate him from his best friend Joel, but their friendship would not suffer and remained as steadfast as the giant oak tree in the park, and like it, it would continue to grow steadily over many years.

Because Moisés needed to help his mother with their daily expenses, he began to search for a job. During this difficult time, he met the visionary José Escobar, a sales and business man who came to the festivities in Moisés's town to make a quick buck selling a bunch of clothing and other items. During this celebration, Moisés worked as a guide for him and helped him with his luggage, which was enough to win José's confidence. This man had a noble soul, and possessed a great business sense and vision. But he also had personal weaknesses; he was a womanizer, a reckless risk-taker and a chain smoker. Since his arrival, he was amazed by the people, the landscape and the aroma emanating from the coffee trees, whose fruit had just ripened. During his stay in the town, Moisés would come to greatly appreciate José Escobar. He treated Moisés like a son rather than a friend. José always gave him the best business advice with the purpose to make Moisés into a successful man. Strangely, however, José forbade Moisés to think of him as an example of success.

With all his flaws and virtues, José decided to settle in the town and start a mattress repair shop, and employed Moisés as his assistant. Soon people sent them mattresses from all over and of all of them different shapes and sizes in order to be fixed. The business gradually began to run smoothly and soon the two of them could no longer meet the customers' orders. When José saw the demand of his business increase, he decided to contract two more employees. So, three months later José created an office for the commercialization of the mattresses, and Moisés became a supervisor. With his new position, Moisés's luck seemed to take a turn for the better. For one thing, he earned a better salary with his new position. However, the momentary happiness he felt in his new position would become overshadowed by his mother's illness. With each day that passed his mother's health deteriorated more and more. The blessing of his new job was just temporary. Just as before, the happiness of the moment would slowly dissipate, as little by little destiny rolled in like a thick fog to unveil a new series of hardships.

Destiny's plot against him would begin to reveal itself the afternoon that Rocio came to the factory looking for him. When she came, Moisés was not there. So, José attended her. When he saw Rocio, he felt an instant connection. It was love at first sight. Those who knew José's desire to seduce women predicted that "the love between them was just a casual feeling". Although the two seemed deeply in love, in time the people who doubted that their love would last turned out to be right. It would seem that Rocio, a brunette with blue eyes, a mermaid figure, and a very noble heart, could find it in her heart to forgive José's betrayals. Her soul's beauty and her abundance of virtues and qualities gave the impression that her love for him was unbreakable. But she was human and therefore flawed. He most pronounced flaw was that she was extremely decisive and never forgave a betrayal. When she said no, it was a resounding no, even when her decision would make her feel like the world was coming down on top of her. Even so, she did not budge an inch.

Moisés and Rocio had always been good friends. She would become his matchmaker and the person who would arrange his clandestine encounters with Mayra, who would become Moisés's first love and the greatest love of his life. When people saw them together, nobody ever imagined that their differing backgrounds would end their relationship. Unfortunately they were wrong. Something soon would happen that would change the course of their love forever. Mayra's father and brother, Manuel, would be the reason for Moisés's newest misfortune. The father found out that his daughter had secret encounters with "The laundress's son" and refused to accept their relationship. Mayra's father, full of wrath, beat his daughter and forbade Moisés from seeing his daughter again. However, neither the beating nor the prohibition could stop the love they felt for each other. In fact, their love only became stronger. The same night of the beating they met again.

However, their encounters would become more and more difficult as each day passed. There was always an informer that would find out and tell the news to Mayra's parents. For that reason, Moisés decided not to see Mayra for a while in order to try and make peace. One day, tired of the situation, he decided to speak with Mayra's father. But "sometimes the cure is worse than the illness", because like a rabid dog, her father attacked him impulsively. As a result, he was left with two black eyes, and a bleeding mouth and nose. This beating not only damaged Moisés's face but his moral. He felt that his life had hit rock bottom. But his love for Mayra was unwavering and he was willing to fight for her with his body and soul no matter the obstacle in his way.

When he got home and his mother saw his swollen and cut face, with worry and distraught etched in her face at the site of her son, she asked:

"What happened hijo?"

Not wanting to worry his mother in her poor state of health, Moisés decided in the moment not to tell her the truth. He paused, quickly inventing a white lie and said: "don't worry mother, I had an accident at work".

That night, after several hours and having recovered from the physical pain of the beating, Moisés returned to Mayra's house. From the window he could see that there wasn't anybody at home. Desperate to have Mayra in his arms, he decided to go look for her. Filled with the desire to divulge his pain to her and find some peace, he walked to all the places where they used to meet secretly, hoping he would find her. However, all his efforts were in vain.

The next day he would receive surprising news from Rocio. When they spoke, she gave him the bitter news that confirmed that Mayra's father had sent her to another city and nobody in the town knew where she was. When Rocio and Joel saw Moisés's sadness, they offered to help him find out where Mayra's parents had hidden their daughter. But everything they did was futile; Mayra's whereabouts was a well-kept secret. A few weeks passed without receiving any news about her, and Moisés began to lose hope. His only source of strength was his mother and his friends, Rocio, Joel and José, who assured him optimistically that at any moment Mayra would come home.

But misfortune would continue to darken Moisés's life. José would soon experience an irreversible tragedy, which would give another twist to his story. Moisés did not know with certainty if José truly loved Rocio or if it just appeared that way on the surface. One afternoon, Rocio came to visit the mattress factory to surprise José. But Rocio was the one who would be most surprised; she found her boyfriend José naked with another woman on a bed, kissing and caressing each other as if they were full time lovers. Seconds after watching that scene, Rocio interrupted the heat of their orgasm. Hurt by the betrayal and with tears cascading down her cheeks, she looked at José in the eye and cried; "Everything is over between us". She swore that as much as she loved him, she would also forget him. José, aware of her feelings of betrayal and disappointment, frantically wrapped a sheet around himself in shame. He then got up, took her by the arm and asked her for forgiveness. Rocio, with her pride wounded, ignored his words; she felt that he had shattered her soul. She turned and ran away, vowing to never see him again.

Hours later, José was desperately looking for someone to help him, his eyes swollen from crying. He regretted his behavior and told Moisés what had transpired. He asked Moisés if he would help him reclaim Rocio's love. Moved by José's painful longing for Rocio, Moisés decided to try and help him, but when he saw the state in which José had left Rocio, he wasn't able to say a positive word about him. He felt that she was right. All he could do was hold her against his chest and offer some comfort while she cried. Although Rocio refused to see him, José remained determined to get her back. He sent her countless letters trying to persuade her that his betrayal was nothing but a moment of weakness and he would never be unfaithful to her again. Desperate for their reconciliation, he gave her flowers, gifts and sang serenades by her window. However, none of this made a difference to her. Although Rocio really loved him, she did not care for his supplications, and she remained firm in her decision. Exhausted from the stress and not noticing any results from his efforts, José eventually gave up, and resigned himself to a life without his love. His new refuge became booze, and it wasn't long before he had become an alcoholic. One afternoon, José locked himself in the factory and began to drink. While the alcohol fogged his mind, the romantic songs that he was listening to made him wallow in the nostalgia of Rocio's love.

Hours later, in the midst of his alcoholic stupor and crying like a child, José forgot a cigarette butt on the side of a cabinet as he collapsed on top of one of the mattresses. A few minutes later, sleep overcame him. As his body relaxed, the cigarette butt simultaneously fell down on some scraps of cotton.It immediately created a flame, which together with the evening breeze soon became a seething fire that hungrily began to consume the entire building. The smell of smoke from the factory penetrated the walls, and would soon alarm all the neighbours, who startled, ran out into the street. They could see the immense column of smoke coming from the factory roof. The fire had overtaken the entire building; someone reminded the others that José was inside the burning factory. In a state of bewilderment, without thinking of the danger, a man decided to shoot down the doors and try to rescue him from the fire. He courageously pulled his unconscious body from the blaze. Although José had received third degree burns in seventy percent of his body, he still retained his vital signs. He was rushed immediately to the town's only Hospital. But, due to the seriousness of his wounds, they would need to send him to the Hospital in the capital.

That morning in the middle of his agony, José gave Moisés his ex-wife's telephone number. While the doctors finished the transfer procedures, Moisés phoned her. When she heard about the tragedy, she became distraught and promised that she would be on the first flight to the capital. That afternoon, when José and Moisés arrived at the hospital, three people awaited them in the hall of the Medical Center. Among them was an older woman who never stopped crying. The other two were a woman of about forty-five and a young man, who at the time would have been almost the same age as Moisés.

Immediately after their arrival, José was admitted into the hospital and brought into the intensive care ward. With his burnt skin, his body had become very delicate. As a result, his state had worsened to the point where even large amounts of morphine didn't relieve his pain. The doctors said that they had done everything possible and even the impossible to save his life. Even so, José's recovery depended on a miracle. That night, they were all anxiously waiting to hear from the doctor about his condition. When the next morning arrived, Moisés left the hospital to look for a hotel room. Fortunately, he found a hotel close to the hospital. While he got some rest, the two women and the young man stayed with José, with the hope that he would react to the medication.

Hours later, all together again and more relaxed, they became confident that José would survive. Then, in the midst of her grief, José's mother approached Moisés and asked:

"Joven!" What's your name?"

He replied breathlessly: "My name's Moisés. With forced composure she answered:

"I'm Angela", and she introduced him to her daughter-in-law Bridget, who introduced him to her son, Charles.

A few seconds later Angela interrupted their conversation and said:

"Sorry Moisés, but with so much anguish, none of us have had time to thank you for all the good you have done for my son". Feeling crushed by the same anguish, Moisés replied melancholically. "Don't worry Señora; it was the least that I could do for him".In the hospital's hallway they continued to wait anxiously for José's recovery.

Meanwhile, back in Moisés's village, Rocio's life had taken a new course. She was a nervous wreck and ridden with guilt due to José's tragic accident. Stifled from her anguish, she could not find peace even in sleep. Her parents didn't feel they had any choice but to bring Rocio to her twin sister's home in another town, hoping that her sister's presence and new surroundings would help her recover from her crisis.

At that time Mayra, Moisés's girlfriend, was also desperately trying to get in touch with him from the boarding school where her parent's had sent her. Clueless to what had happened to José, she wrote Rocio, and in the same envelope sent a hidden message to Moisés. However, Rocio and her family weren't in the village and many of these letters were returned to her. Mayra was very worried and anxious for news from her beloved Moisés, so she sent a letter with Manuel's friend to Mariela, Moisés's mother. But the man betrayed her confidence and gave the letter to Mayra's father instead. Taking advantage of the situation, her father paid the man to lie and give Mayra a false version of events. He told him to assure her that Moisés was with another woman. This shocking news would cause Mayra deep suffering. She would live with a shattered soul for a long time.

While this plot against Moises's happiness had unveiled itself, he remained in the capital, wistfully recalling all of his loved ones in the village as he woke up in the hotel room. He remembers his friends, Rocio, Joel, and Teresa, his former teacher. He also remembered his classmates, his girlfriend and his mother, Mariela. But these memories were fleeting because most of his mind was preoccupied with José. The ringing from Moisés's phone in the hotel room startled him from his thoughts. Seconds later, he would hear the receptionist call out: "Moisés Fernandez!" "please come to the reception, someone wants to speak with you". Immediately he ran to the small room, and answered the call. It was Angela. She notified him that José's state had worsened. Very concerned about the fateful news, he hurried to the hospital with the hope of still finding his friend alive. However, when Moisés arrived, he found Bridget, Angela and her grandson, embraced in sorrow. In the midst of their despair, they exclaimed:

"Moisés, José has passed away!". Moisés felt as if something very heavy had just crushed into his chest. With a sunken heart from the news of his friend's death, he accompanied the others in their pain, and immediately tears began to stream down his cheeks. He had not only lost an employer and friend but the man who was like a father to him, the father that he had never had.

Hours after José's death had been confirmed, a funeral home in the capital got a permit from forensic medicine to take the cadaver, put Jose's corpse into the coffin and bring it to San Carlos Antioquia. There, he would be given a Christian burial. The ceremony to bid him farewell would be a procession accompanied by hundreds of people to the cemetary. He was very appreciated by all of the village residents. When he arrived at the cemetery, a group of Mariachis were playing his favorite songs. Moisés accompanied the mourners to his grave each night as family and friends would gather there for nine nights to place flowers, candles and pray. On the ninth night, after giving his final respects, he packed his suitcase and decided it was time to go. While he was leaving, Angela, José's mother, grateful to him for his loyalty and friendship to José, exclaimed: "Moisés, whenever you want to visit us, there is a place for you here, and if there's something you need, please do not hesitate to call us". Grateful to her for her hospitality, he proceeded to thank them for all their attention during his stay. As he left the apartment, Charles decided to accompany him.

When Moisés returned to his village, the whole town knew that José had passed away, because days earlier Moisés had sent telegrams to his friends about the tragedy. For that reason, many of his friends in mourning came to give him some encouragement, but when they found out that Moisés's companion was the deceased son, their condolences were directed to Charles. The two then took the road towards Moises's house. There, his mother, who had been anxiously awaiting her son's arrival, kissed and embraced him. Immediately after the emotional reception, Moisés introduced her to Charles, José's son.

Minutes later, leaving their suitcases at Moisés's home, they walked back into town. Moisés showed Charles the place where Jose's factory had been, now in ruins. That afternoon, Moisés met his friend Joel near the ruined factory. After giving him a big hug, he introduced him to Charles. Then the three of them, deeply engaged in conversation, went for a walk in the village park. There, Moisés optimistically asked Joel about Mayra's whereabouts. With deep regret he replied: "sorry Moisés but I have no idea where her parents have taken her". When Moisés asked about Rocio, he told her that she was very ill. Since the fateful day that José had been rushed to hospital, she had suffered a nervous breakdown. Her precarious psychological state only worsened when she learned of José's death. Although Rocio loved José in silence, she had refused to give him a second chance. This decision would convince her that she was a disgraced woman and she had become consumed with such enormous guilt that she began to lose her sense of reality. Due to her unstable psychological state, her parents felt they had no choice but to place her in psychiatric clinic for the mentally ill. Moisés, worried about his friend's misfortune, decided to visit her. He hired a taxi to take Charles and him directly to the Psychiatric Center in Ocaña, the town where Rocio was undergoing treatment. He arrived there with the hope that she would be better, but seeing her confirmed everything that Joel had told them. Rocio did not even recognize him, and only stared at him aggressively, speaking to them in incoherent phrases. Moisés, overwhelmed by her confused state wanted to get close to her. However, when he tried to embrace her, she immediately rejected him. Shocked by her strange behaviour, Moisés spoke to the doctor and asked:

"Doctor, why is Rocio behaving this way?"

The psychiatrist explained that her behaviour was temporary and due to her experience of loss. At that moment, Moisés realized the gravity of his friend's situation. But the worst part for him was the inability to do anything for her; he could only pray to God, and ask him for her speedy recovery. When both he and Charles were leaving the Psychiatric hospital, Moisés went to see Rocio's parents, and after greeting them with a big hug, he expressed the sorrow he felt for their daughter. After listening to Moisés, Señor Martin, Rocio's father, focused on the boy beside Moisés. Curiously, he came right up to Moisés's ear and in a loud whisper asked.

"Who is your companion?"

In order to avoid a possible grudge, he introduced Charles as his second cousin. That evening after visiting Rocio, they talked for a long time. Charles, surprised by Rocio's illness, asked about his father José's great love for Rocio, which had ended in such tragedy. Soon, looking at his watch they realized it was time to return.

Back in the village, Moisés visited Joel, who lent him the books to make up for the classes he had missed. Since it was Saturday, Joel could help him with his homework. When he finished, Moisés accompanied Charles to the hotel where his father José had been staying in his final days before the fire. There, he paid the pending bill, collected Jose's belongings and that same day donated them to the town's orphanage. When he came back that night, they met with Elkin and Robert, the factory's employees. Charles paid them what his deceased father owed them. After walking almost all day they were both exhausted and thirsty. They went to a pub, and ordered two drinks. Manuel, Mayra's brother, was there and when he saw them coming, he gave them a wry smile, and exclaimed.

"Look who we have here!" The laundress's son!"

In response to the insult, Moisés decided to ignore him, focusing on his conversation with Charles. While Manuel continued to insult him, Moisés and Charles drank their soft drinks and conversed pretending not to hear him. These words no longer caused Moisés pain as he had become so accustomed to being insulted. However, suddenly Charles rose from his chair and with a defiant tone said: "Show some respect Señor! Act like a person and not a buffoon". Infuriated by Charles's defiance, Manuel approached him and took a swing directly at Charles's face. But before he felt the impact of his fist, Manuel had been taken out and lay flat on his face. He then took on Manuel's friends who in no time also ended up on the floor. Everyone in the bar was impressed with how Charles had defended himself so skillfully against the four aggressors; taking out these guys had been a piece of cake for him.

Completely astonished, Moisés asked:

"Charles, where did you learn to defend yourself like that?"

He explained that since he was a young child he had studied martial arts. He had been influenced by his father, who had been a great karate fighter. Charles was a master black belt and sometimes he gave free Karate lessons. Excited at the prospect of learning martial arts, Moisés eagerly accepted his offer to give him an intensive course for almost three months.

Thereafter, Moisés scheduled his days around his karate classes. In the morning he collected the money from the sold mattresses and looked for new customers, in the afternoon he learned martial arts, and then spent his evenings studying at night school. On Saturdays and Sundays he and Charles would meet Joel on the football field; there he practiced Karate with Charles all morning. After finishing his classes they would all walk around town. During those walks, Charles would talk about his profession, his family and his future. Moisés always talked about Mayra and how they had been separated against their will because of her parents. Sometimes they would interrupt this weekend routine and travel to "Ocaña" to visit Rocio. They maintained hope that she would react to her treatment.

The day before of his departure, Charles asked Moisés to come to the bank with him. There, he opened an account under Moisés's name and deposited three thousand nine hundred Colombian pesos. Immediately after opening the savings account, Charles said: "Moisés, for each mattress sold, you should take 20 percent of your earnings and deposit the rest in your new savings account. When you have a considerable amount, please contact my grandmother and she will tell you what to do. Charles also explained that as an extra gift he would give him the tools and materials rescued from the fire. That evening, Charles announced to Moisés that he would be returning to Medellín early in the morning. He had received an unexpected invitation from the International Committee of karate, and would have to return. The next morning, Mariela got up early to say goodbye to Charles with a kiss on the cheek. He responded to her kind gesture by inviting her to visit him at his house in San Carlos. In addition, Charles gave her the address and phone number in order to communicate with his grandmother if needed. Mariela gratefully reminded him that whenever he wanted to return, he would be well received. Moisés then accompanied him to the bus terminal. With a hearty embrace, Moisés wished Charles the best of luck.

HIS ON-GOING DREAM

During the ensuing months, obstacles continued to obstruct Moisés's path. Despite his misfortunes, he would always pick himself up again; he refused to allow life's difficult circumstances defeat him. He always searched for a better future. His goal at that moment was to start a small factory but, someone with more economic resources stole his idea and beat him to it. This didn't ruin his dream; it simply postponed it. He knew that his life was plagued with the kind of waiting that was beyond his control, forcing him to face every day with courage and patience.

Optimistically, he hoped that his mother would win her battle against her disease. He also hoped he would receive good news from his friend Rocio, Mayra and Charles. He wished with all his heart that Mayra would return and they would be together again. In the midst of all of these hopes, the last of these would almost materialize on the evening he spoke to la Señora Angela.

After an affectionate greeting -Moisés asked about Charles's Karate competition. Excited, she replied that her grandson had made it to the second round in Japan. Amazed by Charles's success, he congratulated her. Immediately after his congratulatory words, he got straight to the point and told her that he was unable to continue in the mattress business. Also, he confirmed that he would send the money the business had earned the following day. When he told her the amount, Angela changed the topic of conversation and asked:

-"Moisés, how are things going in your life?"

Very enthusiastically he answered that he had finished high school and would receive his diploma the following week. That achievement and watching his mother recover a little made him very happy. But at the same time he was deeply disappointed because hadn't received any news from Mayra. Angela, upset by this news said:

-"Moisés, you can't imagine the pain that your sadness causes me. However, you must be strong and go forward because not everything in life will work out the way you want it to."

After her efforts to comfort him, she told him to go to the bank and take five thousand pesos out of the savings account as a gift for obtaining his high school diploma. Moisés, shocked by her generosity exclaimed:

"But Señora, I can't accept it! That's a lot of money!"

Surprised by his answer, she explained:

"If you reject my offer, you would offend my deceased son".

Her generous gift gave him the sense that his luck was going to change.

When his graduation day arrived, he was congratulated by his teachers for his achievement. He had received the highest grades among the graduates in the province. That afternoon, Moisés could not hide his happiness, although it would only be complete with Mayra's presence. He felt enveloped in hope that at any moment she would appear. But that was a mere illusion that would slowly evaporate with the beginning of each new day which would confirm her absence and his loneliness without her.

The evening of his graduation, Moisés was accompanied by his mother who wore a beautiful red dress of fine fabric, making her the most elegant woman of the night. He, like the master of ceremonies, wore a tuxedo of fine fabric, a linen shirt and a pair of Armani black leather shoes. Mariela seemed to have forgotten her delicate state of health and was full of happiness for her son, exhibiting pride in front of all whom were present while Moisés received his diploma. For these reasons, Moisés provoked envy among several of those attending from the upper class. They had expected their son or daughter to achieve the highest grades, not a lower-class kid like Moisés. Because of their deepening envy, which was written on their faces during the ceremony, Moisés knew having a big party at this house would make them even greener. However, his mother's illness prevented him from hosting the party because she needed to sleep the whole night and wouldn't be able to with all the noise. So he and his friend Joel agreed to have a party at his residence with relatives and friends,

That night, before the big fiesta, known in his town as "la rumba", Joel proposed that all of them take a moment of silence to remember José, the person whom Moisés considered his father. Afterward, they began to celebrate with drinks. Although Moisés had never had tequila, that night he drank to get drunk, and in the midst of his drunkenness he wept for Mayra, the woman that he still loved. He didn't care that she might have forgotten him by now.

With these words, Moisés had completed telling this chapter in his life.

A few seconds later, Hansel exhaled, sighing deeply and began to narrate the following chapter of Moisés's life. Very nostalgically he continued:

It was 1982 and at only nineteen years of age, Moisés had been shaken by more than one tragedy. Although he had experienced some joy, he had seen far too much sorrow in his young life. The negative events, however, hadn't undermined the strength of his will that was built on a very solid base, like that of a strong oak tree. Its roots where like the foundations of his character that would support him in the face of his tragedies because no matter what, he wouldn't allow the havoc of adversity uproot him. Certainly, he experienced times of weakness, moments when he couldn't even distinguish a faint light in what seemed like an endless void. But whenever he reached the point of "throwing in the towel", his fighting spirit would manage to find a way out.

A year later, having made the transition from a child to a man, he thought that life would finally change its course for the better. However, his misfortune only worsened and would continue to affect those he loved. This time, destiny's victim would be his friend Joel who suffered a serious accident and was fighting for his life. This incident seemed to confirm to Moisés that his life had been cursed. When he visited his friend at the hospital, he vowed in front of his mother that if Joel died, he would never seek another friendship nor get involved romantically with anyone. He vowed to leave his town forever in order to avoid anyone else being affected by his misfortune or guilt. Fortunately, Joel recovered but destiny would still force Moisés to follow through with part of his promise. He would soon face the moment in his life that he most dreaded: to leave his sick mother alone. Many of his friends claimed that he would be exempt from the military service as the only son and soul supporter of his mother. However, on one particular day, circumstance wouldn't work in his favor.

That day, Moisés got up earlier than usual. There was a shine in his eyes that reflected the joy of a fresh day. With great effort and some luck he had managed to raise enough money to realize his dream of starting his own business. But he was unable to make his desire reality because hours later, against his will, he was recruited by the army. He sailed through the physical exam and was told he would be sent to his post immediately. But following the notification, Moisés refused to join. The recruiter asked him why he should be exempt from the compulsory military service. Moisés argued that as an only child he was financially responsible for his mother. But even more importantly, his mother was very ill couldn't be left alone for a long time. After that, he explained that he had come to the city to start his own business and as proof he showed the army recruiter the money he had hoped to use. However, the recruiter did not believe him, and since there was no one there to defend him, he was forced to be part of a new military contingent.

After listening the Moisés's reasons the recruiter said:

"Sorry, Fernandez, but the only thing I can do for you is escort you to the bank and allow you to send the money back. You can also make a call and explain to your mother what happened. Without choice, Moisés was accompanied by two officials to the Telecom office. From there, he made a phone call. When he talked to his mother, the first thing he did was prepare psychologically. He knew that the bad news could compromise her health. After a few minutes of relaxed conversation he approached the subject cautiously; he told her that he had been recruited by the army and soon would be wearing the army uniform. Her eyes immediately filled with tears and he could hear her crying. Between sobs she told him that she would be there tomorrow. Feeling heartbroken to hear her cry he said: "Mother! I am sad too, but don't worry about me. If you come, I really don't think you could do anything to change what has happened." After this piece of advice he told her to tell to Joel the news. Moisés then assured her that the money that was meant to start his new business would be transferred to her name. He told his mother that it was available to her for anything she needed. Confused, she exclaimed: "What I need is for you to be here! Without you,

I don't know what do with that money!" Moisés assured her that Joel would help her with the money. When Moisés felt her voice had grown calmer, he asked her about his friends, Mayra and Rocio. Mariela replied that she hadn't heard any news from Mayra but that she had received good news about Rocio. "She has recovered and the doctor will release her from the psychiatric hospital next week. Yesterday we talked about you on the phone and when I told her about your new project, she seemed very happy" said Mariela.

When it came time to say goodbye, Moisés reminded her to take his advice and assured her that he would be okay. Before he hung up the phone, he let her know that next Sunday the military base would allow visitors, but if she couldn't visit him, he would try to visit her the following week.

Mariela and Carrillo Deaths

Three days after starting his military service, while Moisés was in the midst of target practice, his sergeant, Roldan, approached him and with a forceful tone, exclaimed.

"Fernandez, you have a visitor, please report to the Command".

Immediately Moisés thought about his mother. But, when he arrived at the office, a surprise was waiting for him. Not only did he find his mom, he also found Joel and Rocio. When his friend Rocio saw him, she ran toward him and hugged him tightly. Moisés then shook Joel's hand and embraced his mother. Together they engaged in lively conversation that lasted for several hours.

Seeing his mother's calm state and Rocio recovered filled Moisés with immense joy and optimism. If someone looked a little concerned, it was Joel. So Moisés approached him and attempted to ask him what was wrong, but before Moisés could open his mouth, Joel said:

"If you're about to ask me about Mayra, I haven't heard anything". Right then, Rocio looked him directly in the eye and contested, "Joel! It would be best if Moisés knew the truth". Surprised by Rocio's words, Moisés implored, "What truth?"

Although Rocio sensed the sadness that her confession would produce in her friend, she replied: "The secret that Joel wanted to hide from you". She paused uncomfortably before continuing. "Although I know what I'm about to tell you will hurt you deeply, it's better you don't maintain any false hope. Mayra met a professor at the University and they recently got married. She was disappointed because she hadn't heard from Moisés in months. Her parents pushed her to marry the professor and eventually she began dating him. She found a kind of refuge in him. But even if you don't believe me, she was desperate to communicate with you for such a long time. She used every medium possible to try and get in touch with you; she tried phoning me at home and sent me letters and telegrams to find out about you. However, no one was ever at home, because I was in the psychiatric hospital and my family had accompanied me. Due to the circumstances, many of her letters were returned to her. Mayra was so desperate to get in touch with you, she even had Manuel's friend take a letter to your mother Mariela. However, he betrayed her and gave the letter to Mayra's father, who subsequently gave him money to lie to her. The man told Mayra that you had left the village, gotten involved in a new relationship and had forgotten her".

Seeing Moisés's deep disappointment, Rocio hugged him again in an effort to comfort him. Then she told him she understood how he felt because like him, she had also lost her beloved. Moisés, trying to sound strong, said. "For months I've had the feeling that she'd forgotten me". Trying to distract Moisés from his loss, Rocio changed the subject to José. With nostalgia she asked about the detail surrounding José's funeral, which had occurred while she was in treatment at the psychiatric clinic.

Moisés divulged everything to her, without omitting any details. He talked to her about José's being transferred to the Cucuta hospital in the Capital, where he had met José's ex-wife, his son and mother. He also mentioned that many people had attended the funeral. Finally, he told her about

Charles, José's son and the fight that had ensued between him and Mayra's brother, Manuel.

Distraught by her memories of José, Rocio asked:

"Does José's family still feel some resentment towards me?"

Moisés was quick to answer: "No, they don't. They're very sympathetic. As proof of their forgiveness, Charles, José's son and I went to visit you three times while you were hospitalized".

Minutes later, it was time to say goodbye and Moisés embraced his mother, kissed her on the forehead and fondly wished her recovery. Just before leaving, Moisés called Rocio and Joel to the side and said, "As you know, my mom has enough money to set up her own business. Since you're my friends, please help her."

A month later, when his mother visited him again, among the many things that they chatted about, she told him that, with the help of Rocio and Joel, she had opened up a store that sold clothing and small appliances. The business was going well, and growing with each day, attracting more and more customers. After their conversation, his mother bid her son farewell and promised him that Rocio, Joel and she would attend the ceremony where he would become a soldier and give his oath to the Colombian flag.

While he waited for this day to arrive, Moisés made a new friend in the Battalion, a–Venezuelan boy with the last name Carrillo. Moisés loved to imitate his Venezuelan accent; they shared the same sense of humour and he learned virtues from Carillo such as humility. Soon they became best buddies.

As their friendship consolidated, their training became much more difficult in the battalion. One day, during an obstacle race, Carrillo suffered an accident. Moisés stopped in his tracks to help him. When he saw that Carillo had dislocated his leg, he picked him up and put him over his right shoulder and carried him to the first aid tent. It didn't matter to him that he had lost several minutes in the competition.

Even so, he ended up winning the obstacle race. Sergeant Roldan praised his courage and that morning in front of the platoon, he recognized Moisés's actions as being exemplary.

In that moment, Moisés attempted to satisfy his curiosity, because he was sure he knew the Sergeant's face from long ago but out of respect he didn't ask him. However, days later, Moisés would figure it out himself. One afternoon in his office, when the Sergeant was giving him a badge of honor for his previous effort, the sergeant asked him: "Where are you from?"

Moisés responded: "I am from a small town called Convención". When the Sergeant heard his answer, his eyebrows lifted in surprise. "I'm from there too!", he exclaimed. At that moment Moisés saw him for the first time without his military hat, and he could distinguish a small scar on his forehead. From this detail, Moisés confirmed who he was without doubt. Positive he was right and returning nostalgically to a time ten years ago, Moisés remembered an event in his childhood. Then he told him melancholically;

"I was the child that you defended one day in the village and because you stepped in, one of my attackers injured you with a stone. The Sergeant meditated for a few seconds, and amazed, he exclaimed:

"Oh! "You're Mariela Fernandez's son!". "Yes Sir, I am", Moisés replied. After a few minutes of reminiscing about of the past, the Sergeant changed the topic of conversation to the present and asked: "How are the officers treating you?"

Moisés replied confidently:

"I don't have any problems with them. The problem is with the older soldiers who always are playing pranks on us. I don't appreciate that some members of our squad are taking our belongings and trying to get us into trouble." The Sergeant explained: "At this stage of recruitment you should be on high alert. You have to give them what's coming to you. If someone robs your personal items, you need to steal from them to ensure you aren't missing anything when the officers come to do their inspection. Don't worry about the other pranks, but make sure you never lose control because they will do their best to get you into trouble." After giving Moisés this piece of advice, the Sergeant asked him with curiosity: "Why have they given you the nickname Bruce Lee in the squad?"

Moisés smiled and replied: "In my free time I practice martial arts. The discipline helps me relax and it's a kind of therapy when I'm feeling down." The sergeant pressed further, "Do you practice it as a hobby?" "Yes", Moisés answered. "Even though my friends claim I'm a Karate instructor, I've never trained at an Academy. I learned Karate from Charles, the son of a friend who passed away. He taught me in my town. By training hard and following the Chinese proverb, "practice is what makes the difference», I progressed quickly."

After their conversation, the day passed according to the usual routine. Moisés had almost completed the recruitment stage and was waiting impatiently for the ceremony where he would become a soldier and make his pledge to the flag. He knew after that, he could return to his town for a while.

At last the day arrived, and Moisés saw Joel, Rocio and his mother who had promised to attend the ceremony. He was seated in front of the stage and waited patiently for them to call his name.

Minutes later, he heard his last name. Once he stepped onto the stage, the Colonel exclaimed enthusiastically: "Soldier Fernandez! The rifle you are given today will be your girlfriend, lover, and an inseparable companion." Moisés then put his right hand on the bible and swore to God that he would defend the Colombian Constitution in any war or conflict. Having completed his pledge, he ran to La Plaza de Armas where the new soldiers met with their family members to celebrate. They were showered with praise and gratitude from the commanders and enjoyed the party wholeheartedly.

The next morning, minutes after the sound of the bugle; Moisés's platoon was called to the building where they stored supplies and took care of logistics. Once he arrived, an officer gave him a duffle bag and three thousand six hundred Colombian pesos. He also received a permit to leave the military base for fifteen-days. In order to warn each of the new soldiers and instill fear in them, the Colonel stated sternly: "Those who do not come back on the stipulated date will be tracked down, brought back and will spend the rest of their military service in a prison cell. After hearing this harsh warning, Moisés met with his relatives and friends, and from there they left for his village.

The evening he arrived home, he saw the date that he had left home written by his mother on the wall, which reminded him that he had been absent from his mother's side for three months and nine days. With his return, Moisés observed the many changes. He witnessed the success of his mother business with his own eyes. Customers were flocking to the store, forcing his mother to consider hiring more employees. Moisés also noticed a growing affection forming between Rocio and Joel. Although their relationship had not been made public, both were secretively in love. According to Rocio, the only drawback was the age difference between them, Joel being six years younger than her. But one evening, while Moisés and Rocio were talking in Mariela's kitchen, Moisés assured her that a difference in age shouldn't matter when you were in love; the feelings they shared was what mattered.

The next day, Moisés went into town and decided he would stop by Rocio's house. Martin, his friend's father, answered the door and invited him in. He told him that he had a letter for Moisés. As Señor Martin opened the cabinet drawer, took it out and handed it to Moisés, he said that he had kept this letter for him for a long time. Señor Martin explained:

"This is one of the many letters that Mayra sent to our address in hope of it reaching you. Unfortunately, nobody was here and the other letters were returned to her. At that moment, Rocio who had made him coffee, came back from the kitchen. When she saw Mayra's letter in Moisés's hand, told him sadly while looking at the letter, "This is the proof that Mayra was desperate to get in touch with you". Feeling confused, and with her letter in his hands, Moisés clung to it for a few minutes without opening it. But then, in a rush of emotion, he decided would not open it and he left it on the table. He thought to himself, Mayra was a closed chapter in his life.

Later that day, Moisés met some former classmates who were very happy to see him. Having experienced many friends that never returned after leaving for military service, they were very curious:

"Is it true", they asked, "what people say about the army - Or just speculation?"

Moisés answered, «The lion is not as fierce as he is painted". He then clarified that the hardest part of his training was over. He promised them that next time he came to visit he would have a lot more to tell them.

Two days before returning to the battalion, Moisés, his mother, Rocio and Joel went to see the movie «The game of death» starring Bruce Lee. That movie was an apt farewell, as the following morning he would be returning to the barracks with unknown battles ahead of him. The time of his departure arrived, and with nostalgia for his loved ones written on his face, Moisés hugged each of them goodbye with tears in his eyes. Then he kissed his mother and promised her that he would be in contact every weekend and would be returning home on Christmas day.

He arrived at the Capital on Sunday afternoon with some time to spare since he didn't have to be at the barracks until Monday. So to pass the time, he decided to go to the shopping centre, Alexandria Plaza. There, after purchasing a few personal items, he went to the local café to have refreshment. At that moment he heard someone call out his name. "Fernandez!" "Fernandez!" When he turned around, he saw Carrillo Edwin, his buddy, with an elegant blonde woman. Carrillo introduced him to his girlfriend, and invited Moisés to come over to his house and spend the night with his family in their town. Carillo's girlfriend drove and took the Cucuta's highway and when they were passing by the town, Villa Del Rosario, she stopped and parked the car at a viewpoint. There in a restaurant, they ordered the house specialty. While they waited for their food to arrive, they drank a few beers. They had such a fun time that they were astonished when they realized that it was past midnight. They got back into the car and continued their trip to the border. On the journey, having crossed into Venezuela, Carillo pointed out to Moisés the Venezuelan landscape now bathed in moonlight. Soon dawn's first light would cast an array of pinks and yellows on the horizon. Finally they arrived at Edwin Carillo's house around four in the morning where Moisés was welcomed warmly by the Carillo family.

They went directly to sleep and weren't roused until late morning by sound of children playing outside. They had a leisurely breakfast and then Edwin's father drove them back to the battalion. On the drive, his father told Moisés that he had tried to provide Edwin with a good and easy life. He wanted to buy him a military card that would exempt him from mandatory military service, but his son had refused. Then he paid for his studies at university but Edwin had left midway through the program, without finishing his degree. He also got Edwin to join cadets with the purpose of pursuing

a military career, but he didn't like it. "Without doubt, Edwin
is a rebellious kid" lamented his father. "He ended up opting
for compulsory military service just to go against my wishes!
But since he is the youngest child, I wasn't too hard on him
and in time, I accepted his decision." Moisés pondered Señor
Oscar's words, and after a short silence he said:

"My situation was completely opposite from Edwin's.
I was forced to become a soldier and had no other option."
Carrillo›s father said. "That's the paradox of life; some of us
have everything and don't know what to do with it or worse,
squander it, and others, like you, have little and would do
anything for more options and the opportunity to achieve
your goal".

Minutes after their conversation, they arrived at the
battalion. Moisés and Carrillo immediately signed themselves
in to the guard Commander, who ordered them to go to their
former Squadron. Shortly upon their arrival they were thrown
back into training, learning new strategies and military tactics.
These techniques incorporated defense skills, such as how to
handle and disable explosives, and when one should retreat in
case of an ambush.

At the battalion, the days passed without incident. Although
they did not yet have to test their skills, they knew that they
were being prepared to face future battles. In those days of
peace, Moisés thought that destiny had changed course and
was now in his favor. However, this was not so. Months earlier
a new plot was building against him, gaining ground each
day. And as always, it would unleash its fatal consequences,
not on him directly but on the people he loved most. It was
ironic and incomprehensible how fate would strike him where
he was most vulnerable; harming those he was closest to and
subsequently making his suffering unbearable.

However, at that moment Moisés was enjoying some welcome success in his life. One day in the barracks a high ranking officer, a Lieutenant colonel, gave them unexpected news. He ordered all regular privates who had a high school diploma to come forward. Those with the diploma, including Moisés and Carillo, immediately followed the Lieutenant's order and one by one they proceeded to the front of the hall. Of all the troops, there were only a total of eight regular soldiers who came forward, among whom were Moisés and Carrillo. Then the Colonel approached them and in front of the platoon, granted them badges and application forms that assigned them their new rank of third corporal. Immediately after awarding them their new rank, the colonel explained to each of them the benefits of their new rank as third corporals. The badge they had just received, he affirmed, would only be permanent if they chose to fill out the application form and were interested in pursuing a military career. Moisés and Carrillo acquired a fresh attitude in their new role. Very pleased by his new rank, Moisés phoned his mother from a telephone booth to relate the good news. Full of happiness she exclaimed: "!Congratulations hijo! Your achievements make me feel very proud."

During their conversation, his mother confessed to him that lately she had been suffering from migraines, which were worrying her. The doctor already had done some tests and while she was waiting for the results, he advised that she rest. His mother Mariela promised him that as soon as she knew the diagnosis, she would call him at the battalion. Before hanging up the phone, Moisés told her to say hello to his friends, and send a hug to Rocio and Joel.

The news he received from his mother troubled him and instilled an unsound feeling; however, trying not to focus on her diagnosis, he put all his energy toward his training, and tried to forget about his premonition. That afternoon, after returning from training and while in the shower, Moisés noticed two older soldiers in the distance going into his barrack. When he got there, he saw that several shells were missing from his bag. He decided not to make a scandal of it and follow Sergeant Roldan's advice that if someone robs you, you have to "return the favor". So, he went to the older soldiers' barracks, rummaged through their bag and took back what he was missing. He also brought a little extra ammunition back with him, just as a precaution. Although Moisés didn't feel good about this practice in the battalion, he couldn't do anything to change it. It was an established tradition and he had no choice but to adapt to the circumstances. So from the time his companions had first stolen his belongings, he began to do the same in order to avoid being punished. Carrillo was the only one who Moisés trusted because he was his best buddy and like a brother; he would always respect and try to protect his belongings.

Three months after Mariela's medical tests, there had been little change in her condition. The doctors' inability to diagnosis her case confounded and concerned everyone. While the doctors were seeking the cause of her strange illness, back in battalion, life had taken a new course. Colombia was in a territorial dispute with Venezuela, in the "Gulf of Coquibacoa" in the province of Maracaibo and their country was preparing to defend its sovereignty. For this reason, the Minister of Defense ordered a military operation on the border.

In the deployment of platoons, Moisés was sent in a squadron of tanks called "Los cascabeles", a name that refers to a kind of rattlesnake. These tanks and troops were sent to make a clear statement to Venezuela regarding Colombian sovereignty. There, the Colombian troops spent their days on maximum alert, ready to employ their military tactics at any moment. On the other side of the border, they assumed that the Venezuelan soldiers were doing the same since there still had been no sign of an attack. Several weeks passed in a tense calm between both armies. However, one day the Venezuelan army unexpectedly moved their troops out into the open. The Colombian forces believed that an attack was imminent and advanced their troops into a position of combat. But then the dispute was suddenly resolved through international diplomacy. With a signed agreement, the order came to withdraw and for each squadron to return to their respective base.

When Moisés arrived at the battalion he reported to the Commander and a few minutes later, was surprised by Sergeant Roldan, who gave him a telegram from Rocio sent two days earlier. Moisés, stricken with fear at what he would find, opened the envelope with trepidation and began to read. The telegram only said: "Moisés, please call me. It's urgent".

Sensing the worst, he emerged from the office and walked to the Bureau of officers. In the phone booth, he introduced the coins into the machine and dialed his mother's store. It wasn't his mother's voice he would hear at the other end of the line, but if heard his friend Joel's voice. After greeting his friend, he immediately sensed the distress in Joel's voice and asked:

"What's happening with my mother?"

Joel replied:

"I'm so sorry Moisés, but Mariela's condition worsened two days ago; she is in the hospital in the Capital where a specialist is examining her. According to the latest doctor's report, your mother's illness is very serious; the best thing to do is to prepare ourselves for the worst. However, the physicians who are taking care of her are doing everything possible to save her life. Although her vital signs remain stable, the doctors have lost hope of a possible recovery. Rocio is with her. Whatever happens, remember we are hoping for her condition to improve and if there's any change, I will call you immediately."

That night as Moisés lay in bed, Joel's words echoed in his mind like an ominous cassette that replayed itself over and over again, robbing him of sleep. Moisés watched the sunrise haunted by the bad omen that beset him. The sadness in his eyes reflected the deep pain in his soul. But duty called despite his suffering and he had no choice but to start his day with the usual tasks and routines of being a guard. During the ensuing hours on guard he turned his thoughts inward and began to analyze his life. He didn't understand how destiny could be so merciless to harm all the good people around him, his mother being no exception.

His thoughts were interrupted by a soldier who summoned him to Sergeant Roldan's office, where he was requested due to an urgent phone call. In a daze he made his way to Roldan's office to answer the dreaded call. It was Rocio, who breathlessly bewailed:

"Moisés, I'm so sorry, I can't express the sadness that I feel in my soul. I'm so sorry to be the bearer of bad news, but I have no choice but to tell you. You need to know that your mother passed away this morning!"

Moisés felt his body shudder and within seconds tears streamed down his cheeks. His legs felt like leaden blocks molded into the floor, as though he were paralyzed. It was almost impossible to take steps. Stunned, Moisés faltered into the Colonel's office. After greeting him, he conceded to him his sad news. Then he asked permission to attend his mother's funeral. The Colonel denied him the permission to leave, however Sergeant Roldan entered the office at that very moment and intervened in his favor, managing to convince the Colonel to grant him the permission to attend his mother's funeral.

Rocio and Joel arranged the funeral services since it would take him two days to reach his town. When Moisés arrived at his house, his mother already lay in her coffin. They had a vigil that night with him, his two best friends by her side and his mother's friends, who came one by one to pay their condolences. Devastated by her early departure from this world, Moisés drew near to Mariela's coffin and gazed at her face for several minutes. Her image would be imprinted in his memory forever.

Many people came to Mariela's funeral; her humility had earned the respect of the whole town, including those who had not treated her well in the past. Because of this, on the last day of the Novena, the nine days of mourning, something unusual would happen to Moisés. That night, Señor Rafael, a man around forty years of age, who was very well off and known to everyone as Moises's father, approached him. For the past twenty years of Moisés's life this man had never shown any interest in him.

Rafael, remorseful for Mariela's death and for having been an absent and neglectful father, attempted to engage in conversation with Moisés and in the midst of his monologue, he asked:

"Do you know who you are talking to?"

"Yes, of course" Moisés said. "You're Señor Rafael Quintero". With a surprised look on his face he replied:

"I'm not just Rafael Quintero! I am your father." Disgusted, Moisés uttered vehemently: "My father? You have never spent a minute of your time with me, so I don't understand why you think you have the right to call yourself my father. To me you died the day I was born."

Rafael apologized, attempting to make amends for his mistakes. Rattled and with a lump in his throat he replied:

"I'm so sorry Moisés, but today I am here and I'd like to help you."

Full of courage Moisés answered:

"You should have given me the support you're offering now nineteen years ago. It's too late now". Those words left Rafael at a loss for words, and with his pride wounded, he walked away.

When Moisés had reached this point in his story, I was so moved that I couldn't stop myself from interrupting him with a burning question:

"What disease killed your mother?" I inquired.

Moisés, enveloped in nostalgia responded:

"My mother died young, at only 39", and according to the medical doctors, she suffered from an unknown disease. Her metabolism produced small doses of lead continuously that little by little were accumulating in her heart and would eventually end her life. The doctors were confused and didn't understand how this metal was being produced in her body!"

Her diagnosis was an enigma for a long time. Only many years later, a toxicologist who was intrigued by the strange disease that had caused her death, studied her medical history and discovered the source of her illness. According to the forensic report, there had been an error made by a surgeon. I you remember, years earlier she had been impacted by two bullets, but during the surgery the surgeon had only found one. The other projectile, after entering her body, had stayed in the patella of her knee. Since this bullet was not in a place that caused her pain, and fairly close to the other bullet, it went unnoticed and the surgeon and my mother, didn't know that a bullet was still there. Every day the friction caused by walking would send small particles of lead into her heart, which produced her illness and led to her death."

At that moment he added sarcastically:

"The irony was that the bullet, which had only caused a slight wound in Mariela's body would cause her eventual death. It was one of the many ironies that life's misfortune inflicted upon me, always hurting the people I loved most".

Moisés sighed, tried to dry his tears and cleared his throat, because his nostalgia had produced a lump there.

Minutes later, managing to gain control over his emotions, Moisés took a deep breath and returned to his story, which I'll continue telling now.

After his time at home with friends and family grieving his mother, still exhausted from the emotion of his loss, he had no choice but to return to the battalion and report to his commander. Once he arrived at the barracks, he was plagued by negatives thoughts, feeling that his life no longer had meaning. He began to take unnecessary risks and sometimes acted recklessly. For a long time he wouldn't care about the consequences of his decisions on the present or future.

The afternoon when Moisés arrived at the battalion, his friend Carillo approached him, paused and with an expression of sadness in his eyes gave Moisés a hug and his condolences.

A few seconds later, Carrillo told Moisés that during his absence he had gotten into serious trouble. One evening he was assigned to ensure public order during a party in the city and by chance he ran into his girlfriend who had come to the party with some friends. As soon as she saw him, she ran into his arms and full of emotion kissed him passionately. Immediately, she put a bottle of brandy in his jacket pocket. Without thinking, Carillo began to sip the brandy and an hour later, decided he better have some mints to cover the alcohol on his breath. But the brandy had already gone to his head. Without considering the consequences of his actions, he went up to the table where his girlfriend sat. But at that moment someone moved in front of him to ask her to dance. When she refused, the man became upset and started to insult her. Hearing this man mistreat his girlfriend ignited rage in Carrillo, who under the effects of alcohol, without a single word, hit the man in the face with the butt of his rifle. The hit fractured the man's jaw. As a result, Carrillo was arrested by the military police, and as punishment for his behaviour, he was confined to a prison cell until the facts were clarified.

After hearing about the incident, his father got in touch the man who Carrillo had hit and offered to pay him if he agreed to drop the charges. The man agreed and a few hours later, Carrillo was released from the cell. However, his Sergeant explained to him that in military terms, his lack of discipline would mean that he no longer would receive their support or help, what they referred to in the Colombian military as "el palo cagado". That meant if he ever had a serious problem again, the Sergeant would refuse to help him even if he wanted to, as these were the rules imposed by their superiors.

Several days after that episode, some changes were made in the Battalion. Moisés joined the public order squadron that would be mobilized in the town of Tibú in order to provide security for the coming presidential election. From then on, his squad would be a mobile unit that never stayed in the same place for more than four days. After many comings and goings, Moisés returned to the barracks where Carrillo continued with difficulties. But this time he had family problems. He told Moisés about his ailing mother who he was unable to visit. The Commander would not grant him permission to visit her as punishment for his previous actions. During their conversation, Carrillo also told him that the Commander was selecting soldiers to take a course in order to become a bodyguard. Carrillo then reached into the pocket of his army jacket and pulled out an envelope wrapped in a plastic bag and gave it to Moisés. The letter was from Rocio and Joel. Before opening it, Moisés realized that he had forgotten all about them, having been preoccupied with the tasks at hand. Immediately upon opening the letter, he saw that it was an invitation to their wedding. Thrilled by the news, Moisés phoned Rocio first thing the following morning in order to congratulate her. He expressed his happiness for them but at the same time he felt disheartened because he wouldn't be able to attend. His military obligations wouldn't allow it.

However, he promised her that at his first opportunity to obtain permission to leave he would come see them.

Besides receiving the surprise wedding invitation, everything else would remain as usual in the Battalion. That is, the calm would persist until a fateful afternoon when his buddy Carrillo would make the fateful decision to end his life. This terrible decision, ironically, would be based on a lie made up by his family. They thought that the only way to get the Commander to grant Carrillo a permit to attend a special family event, his parents silver wedding anniversary, would be to make up a lie to convince him. They wanted all their relatives to be present, especially their son, in order to share in their joy on such a special occasion. Since Carrillo's father knew that Edwin had been denied permission to leave previously, he decided to send a note to the Commander with the news that Carrillo's mother was dying. He hoped this lie would soften the officer's heart and convince him to give authorization to his child. However, the Commander denied the permission once again.

Meanwhile, Carrillo really believed that his mother was dying. The inability to visit her produced such anguish that in the midst of his anger and desperation, he impulsively grabbed his Galil rifle and shot himself in the head. The shot blew his brain apart and would also shatter his parents' happiness and well-being from that day forward. That day, Moisés's buddy died believing that his mother was really dying. In order to pay respect to the mourners, the battalion Commander changed the facts and declared that Carrillo had died in the line of duty. His final farewell was made with military honors, where soldiers fired their rifles into the air beside his coffin, which was wrapped in the Colombian flag.

A Hell Called "Miranda"

The day after Carrillo's tragic death, Sergeant Roldan told Moisés that he should report immediately to the Colonel's office. The Colonel welcomed Moisés into his office and told him to immediately collect his belongings because he had been selected to take the bodyguard course at the Miranda military base.

Moisés began his training still distraught by his friend's death, and as he had come to expect, several challenges would accompany him on his new mission. This time the problem would be his height since ninety percent of the applicants were tall. Each of them averaged about a meter eighty. He was teased incessantly and called the tiny soldier. They thought he couldn't possibly bear the arduous task of being a bodyguard. But they were wrong, and many of those who made fun of his short stature, days later would give up the course because they couldn't withstand the difficult training. Even those who stayed complained about their aching muscles continually. Moisés on the other hand, maintained his strength from the beginning. He was acutely aware of his strength and resilience while training and noticed the others growing envy. With resignation they began to treat him with respect and those who remained in the course even began to look at him as an inspiration. He would encourage his classmates so that they could obtain their objectives. So Moisés, due to his own merits, little by little defied his classmates' belief that he was weak and inept due to his short stature and soon he became the leader of the entire course. His classmates always paid attention to his opinions and treated Moisés like an instructor who helped them overcome the physical obstacles of the course. However, Moisés was disheartened to see that with each passing day there were fewer and fewer participants at the Miranda military base. He recalled that the course had begun with fifty soldiers and ended with only thirty-six. On graduation day, several of those soldiers came up to him and congratulated him for his bravery. But his courage was also highlighted by non-commissioned officers and superiors at the base. Moisés was well aware that getting through the course had been arduous. The long days of exhausting training made it seem like there were forty hours in each day! Today the memories of this particular odyssey were contained within a medal of merit, which he stored in a photo album. Whenever he looked it, he realized that no accomplishment was impossible.

The morning after he completed the course, Moisés was transferred to the department of intelligence to be the "V-DOS", Lieutenant Rodriguez's personal bodyguard. Although the attacks on the Lieutenant were sporadic, he and those around him faced moments of great risk. He remembered experiencing the first terrorist attack the afternoon the Lieutenant attended a meeting for the Security Council. On that particular afternoon, while leaving the venue, the convoy was intercepted by a mercenary commando that was working for the cocaine-mafia.

Minutes before the attack, all had seemed placid. No suspicion was initially alerted when a van parked about fifteen meters in front of them, and another appeared at about the same distance, but in the back alley. Both vehicles were being driven by elderly ladies, driving suspicion away; especially when simultaneously both women got out of their cars and walked to different places. None of the bodyguards at the time imagined that other people were hidden in the vans. Then, a motorcycle with two hit men careened into the parking lot. They instantly began firing into the air in order to distract the bodyguards so that their accomplices could achieve their objective of killing the Lieutenant from the second floor of the building and from inside the vans. Moisés, who cautiously observed the elderly women's movements, was the only one who instinctively understood the aggressors' strategy. So, when the Lieutenant came out of the building and approached the armored vehicle, Moisés perceived the accomplices in the van from the corner of his eye and anticipated their attack by shooting first, not allowing his attackers to get a good shot at the Lieutenant. He therefore managed to get the boss into the armored car safely. The terrorists failed attempt immediately put their plan "B" into action. So when the armored vehicles started to move, the van from the back alley tried to block them and the hidden occupants fired shots at them. At the same time, the other van came from behind and sped towards them in order to sandwich them between the two vans. Moisés accelerated towards the vehicle in front of them and was able to swerve to the left, hitting the right flank of the van and making their car spin as it merged onto the highway. The second armored car with bodyguards then intercepted the vehicle that was pursuing them, which initiated a violent confrontation in which a couple of the attackers were killed while trying to flee their vehicle that had turned into a neighborhood.

Three months after this attack, they would be ambushed again. On that occasion, two bodyguards died and three were wounded, including Moisés, who was impacted by several gunshots to his body. That day, minutes after protecting the Lieutenant from the attackers, Moisés would be sent to the military Hospital where a surgeon extracted the bullets. Due to the gravity of his wounds, the surgeon gave Moisés time off in order to heal from his injuries. Once he had recovered, Moisés completed his compulsory military service as a bodyguard, and retired from the military with honors for demonstrating excellence during his service.

Having finished his time in the Colombian army, Moisés departed the military base for home with the intention to finally fulfill his promise to visit Rocio and Joel. The day he arrived home, he planned to surprise them but he ended up being the one most surprised. During the months that he had been absent major changes had taken place. His late mother's business was unrecognizable, transformed into a department store where people bought clothes, shoes and all kinds of electrical appliances. Among these one could find the most sought after novelty of the time: colour TVs, which were being smuggled illegally from the Brazilian border.

When Rocio showed him in the establishment, her eyes shone with pride. She gave him a kiss on the cheek and embraced him. Then, excitedly she told him that they had named their new son Moisés, in honor of him, and their great friendship. At that moment of tenderness, Joel arrived, amazed by Moisés's return and greeted him with a hug. Together the three of them spoke about the good news. Rocio and Joel took advantage of the moment and asked:

"Moisés! Would you like to be our son's godfather?"

Feeling honored, he told them he would accept but on one condition; that they would give the child another name since he believed the name "Moisés" would destine the child to a life of hardship. He told them that they should choose a more modern name like that of a Hollywood actor, a famous singer or a soccer player. In the end, they opted for a soccer player's name, choosing Diseur, the name of a Brazilian soccer star. Then they told him that his mother's former business had been very successful and had enjoyed very good profits. Part of this money, they added, had been deposited in an account under

Moisés's name. Then they showed him the bank statements, so he could verify the amount of interest he had accumulated up to the present date.

Hours later, Moisés visited Mariela's gravestone. When he arrived, a surprise was awaiting him. It was the anniversary of Mariela's death and that evening he found his friends gathered around her tombstone singing songs from mass in homage to his late mother. This humble detail made that him weep for joy.

The days passed and with the elapse of time, the date of the baby's baptism came upon them. The godmother was Joel's cousin who was spending her vacation with them. The morning that Joel introduced his cousin to Moisés, the chemistry was instant. However, despite the chemistry he realized this was not the moment in his life to begin a relationship. He still didn't know what course his life was taking. So, in order to avoid playing with her feelings, he resisted the opportunity to really get to know her. His usual placid spirit had transformed; now he sought danger and adventure.

That's why one morning while Moisés was reading the local provincial newspaper, an unusual classified ad, which read: "Multinational Security Company seeks an employee to make trades involving high risk" drew his attention. He was attracted to the job description because of the danger involved and sent his resume immediately. He attached a note clarifying that he wasn't living in the Capital, but in case of being accepted they could contact him by phone and he would be available to start at any time. The next day in the afternoon, Moisés received a phone call. It was the secretary of the company he had applied to. The women on the phone announced: "Congratulations Señor Moisés, you have been selected to work with us. We would like you to start immediately".

Hours later, Moisés bid his friends goodbye and began his journey to the Capital. He arrived at his new job the next morning. However, when he saw that the position he was offered at the company was to deliver soft drinks, he thought that the supervisor must have made a mistake. He clarified that had applied to a job that required risk and danger. The manager explained to him that the route he would have to take was considered to be precarious, and the company was seeking a person with his abilities. After taking a moment to consider the supervisor's words, Moisés decided to sign the contract. The Chief of staff handed him the keys to a Chevrolet truck, model eighty three, and two assistants were assigned to drive the south east route.

Moisés's new job gave him a new perspective on life. He found his personality suited the job and soon he became the most popular salesman among the customers. They found him to be friendly and someone to whom they could tell there jokes. One afternoon, Moisés would become even more popular. He was eating a piece of cake, when four individuals approached him armed with large knives. It took Moisés a moment to realize he was being robbed. He instantly put all his martial arts training to test and within a few minutes managed to disarm all of them. His courage would be celebrated on the front page of a local newspaper.

Moisés loved his new job. His trips were fun and full of risk, and he found the job very satisfying. In the evenings, Moisés would reflect upon the experiences each day brought him. He came to the conclusion that there would always be difficulty, even within times of happiness. He then recalled one particular morning while he was making a delivery in the city. He had stopped at a traffic light behind two guys on a motorcycle who had pulled up beside a gray limousine. A few seconds later, one man got off the motorcycle and placed a package on the hood of the vehicle and then his accomplice threw a device under the car and took off, weaving through traffic. Immediately, Moisés understood that he was witnessing an attack on the members in the limousine because when the driver tried to move forward, the vehicle suddenly ignited in flames. The next minutes seemed to pass in slow motion. From his truck Moisés realized that there was a bomb in the package that would explode the moment the flames reached it. The imminent danger had paralyzed everyone; the pedestrians fled the scene in search of refuge and no one dared emerge from their cars. Moisés, who had experience with explosives, stepped out of his truck and with calm determination attempted to put out the flames emanating from the vehicle with a fire extinguisher he had in his truck. But it would not be enough, because the front tires were still ablaze. So, he took a couple of liters of coca cola he had and spilled the contents onto the front tires. This managed to extinguish the fire and most importantly prevented the bomb from going off. Having controlled the fire, he pulled the bomb out of the package and with a small flat screwdriver defused it. Meanwhile, the people inside the limousine remained in danger of suffocation because the vehicle doors were sealed shut and the smoke inside began to engulf them in black billows. Moisés instantly grabbed a jack from his truck in order to pry open the back doors. From the back seats he pulled out a women and child. The woman was in shock and the child, who clung to the woman, was crying inconsolably. Moisés then dragged the driver and passenger out of the front seats. Both men were showing symptoms of suffocation and although they were unable to speak, the expression in their eyes showed immense gratitude.

When the police and firefighters arrived, Moisés had gained control over the situation. An ambulance arrived and the occupants of the vehicle were taken to the nearest hospital. Minutes after his heroic act, Moisés reported the details of the attack and his efforts to the police and continued with the day's deliveries. That night, when Moisés arrived at the company office to report his sales, the news of his feat had reached the entire staff. Astounded by his bravery, they celebrated his act of courage, treating him like a hero. Although many reporters wanted to write a story about his heroism, Moisés refused interviews; he didn't want to provoke any possible acts of retaliation.

The next morning, when Moisés walked into the company office, he received an order to see his boss. A big surprise awaited him. There, standing in front of him was the man he had saved from the limousine. It turned out the man was a partner of the company where Moisés worked. His boss immediately introduced the man, Federico Duarte, to Moisés. Federico wanted to thank him for his act of heroism and very humbly, his voice choked with emotion, said:

"Yesterday you saved my wife Marlene and my son Willy's lives, along with mine and my driver's. Your act of courage has made me so deeply grateful to you that no words can express how I feel. In appreciation for your bravery, I would like to give you this blank check, which you can fill with any amount you wish".

Moisés, well aware of Federico's high position in the company, answered surprised:

"Oh Señor! Thank you so much, but I cannot accept it. What I did wasn't meant for profit; It was an act of solidarity that I would do again for you or anyone." Don Federico looked at him with admiration:

"I see that you are not only a brave man, but a great person too. I need someone like you by my side, therefore I would like you to be responsible for my personal safety. Without a hint of smugness, Moisés replied:

"I'm sorry Señor, but I already have a job and signed a contract with the company." Federico immediately replied:

"The contract is not a problem!" If you'd like, I can have these clauses changed".

His proposal left Moisés deep in thought. Although he was very happy as delivery man, he saw this new job as an opportunity to intervene in this man's destiny. Moisés knew that he had honed the skills to perceive imminent threats from criminal gangs and could likely prevent another tragedy. So with the challenge to alter Federico's fate, Moisés accepted his offer.

The first thing that Moisés did was investigate the motive behind the attacks. Federico told him that several years ago a very well organized criminal gang had blackmailed him. Tired by so many demands for his money, he had made an agreement with the DAS officers, and the day that he was supposed to deliver the last extortion payment, the DAS officers had captured the head of the gang. Due to cooperating with the authorities, the rest of the bandits retaliated and sent him death threats. The DAS chief assigned several bodyguards to him and his family, but after one year of protection Federico believed that he and his family were no longer in danger and relaxed the security measures. Two days after that erroneous decision, the criminals made their attack. Thanks to Moisés's actions, their family managed to escape with their lives and tell their story. Moisés recalled that at the very moment Federico was uttering these words, they were interrupted by the doorbell.

Seconds later, one of Federico's employees opened the door and standing there, was one of the most beautiful women Moisés had every laid his eyes upon. She said "hi" to everyone from the doorway. From the moment he heard the woman's voice, Willy, Federico's son, who was expecting her, raced into her arms. Moisés, captivated by her gaze and astonished by so much beauty, glanced over at Federico and asked him discreetly.

"Who is the stunning woman?" Federico replied:

"She's Willy's nanny". They approached each other; Moisés looked at her with a sparkle in his eyes. When Federico introduced her to him as Willy's nanny, she extended her hand out to him and like a medieval knight, Moisés held her hand and kissed her wrist. Then, very gallantly, he said.

"Hello beautiful lady. It's so nice to meet you. My name's Moisés. With a shy smile, the young woman answered:

"I'm Jessica and the pleasure is mine".

Flattered by her warm response, Moisés added: "Your name is beautiful, just as it's owner"

Jessica smiled demurely:

"See you later", she said.

After the pleasant exchange, Moisés continued conversing with Federico. They discussed the route they would drive and details concerning the safety of his family. Moisés advised him to get two escort cars and several more bodyguards. He would need them in case of a possible retaliation from the criminal gang. He also advised Federico to purchase another armored limousine of similar model and color. These cars would serve as protection for them and at the same time, with two identical cars they could confuse the criminals as to which one held the desired passenger. With his strategy in place, Moisés then spoke with Federico's driver and started to teach him some necessary defense strategies and tactics. Among these were learning how to react when a vehicle obstructs the road, how to handle weapons, what to do in the situation of a bomb, and how to react in case of a large scale attack. Immediately after training the driver, Moisés clarified to him that if anything of these scenarios should occur, he should never stop the limousine. Also, he told him that he should rotate the use and positions of the vehicles when Federico was being transported. Federico would sometimes use the limousine parked in the back and other times, the ones in the front. He also emphasized the importance of travelling on streets that weren't busy and to change the route every day.

Although Moises's new job was dangerous he didn't find it too stressful and even more relaxing than his delivery job. The most challenging aspect of the job was providing security for little Willy. He was hyperactive and always on the go. So making sure he wouldn't get hurt was more work than being a bodyguard for his father. Although very restless, Willy was an adorable boy and Moisés soon became very fond of him. Little by little, the boy also grew to like Moisés. He always felt joy around the boy, partially because it was a way to spend time with his nanny, Jessica. With each day that passed, Moisés's affection for her bloomed.

Sometimes when Federico was at home, Moisés guarded Federico's wife, la Señora Marlene as everyone called her. She had the reputation of being a petulant woman among most of her employees. However, since the day she had been attacked by the criminal gang, she had transformed completely. Her metamorphosis came as a surprise to the family, and according to them, it seemed as if she had become another person entirely.

The Decision and Jessica's Tragic End

Moisés's new profession as a bodyguard was filled with both joyous and dangerous experiences. However, only a few months into his new job, misfortune would cast a dark shadow over his life again when the happiest event of his life would turn into a great tragedy.

His duties as Federico's bodyguard included visits to casinos, restaurants, expensive hotels and fancy bars with. Soon Moisés had established good relationships with many of Federico's friends, all of whom belonged to the upper strata of society. In this elite social scene Moisés met many women, and with a couple of them he had romantic flings. These romances were just for fun though, because his mind and soul were focused on winning Jessica's heart. Since he had met her, he had grown to love her intensely. Although Jessica had not yet agreed to become his girlfriend, Moisés refused to give up hope. She would always tell him that she would agree to go on a date the day he was serious about her.

On mother's day his wish became a reality. On that special day, both of them were at Federico's home when Jessica asked Moisés to come walk in the garden with her. There, whispering into his ear, she tenderly said: "Moisés! Tonight I'd like to go to dinner with you". It took a few moments for Moisés to realize what she has said. Moisés was elated. Together they chose a restaurant and the time they would meet that evening. At the restaurant that night, as they enjoyed a delicious meal,

Jessica told him that for several days she had been thinking about their relationship and becoming his girlfriend. She admitted that she had some fears of becoming involved with him because of the dangers inherent in his job; she didn't want her future children to grow up without a father. That comment made her blush; however, with a smile she made light of her embarrassment. Moisés looked at her earnestly. "The day you decide to become my wife, I'll give up this job," Moisés said.

A couple days after their romantic evening, while accompanying Federico to a business lunch, the criminals who had been harassing his boss would attempt to take them by surprise. Fortunately, Moisés and his men reacted immediately. While defending Federico, he and another bodyguard killed two of their attackers. Another of their accomplices was wounded in the leg. They grabbed him and Moisés immediately handcuffed him, covered his face and pushed him up against the side of the car. He applied a tourniquet to the bandit's wounded leg. Judging by the shaking in the criminal's body, he was terrified of being killed. Overcome by fear, he would betray his partners in crime minutes later, in hope that Moisés and the other bodyguards would spare his life. When he told them who he was, Moisés realized that he belonged to the same criminal group that had attacked Federico almost two months earlier. Because of his confession, it would become their lucky day. The DAS squad was close by, and after an intense round of shooting, they captured the rest of the gang.

Not long after this event, Moisés decided to go back to his village to spend his vacation where he visited Rocio, Joel and Dirseur, his godson. He arrived a few weeks before Christmas and spent an unforgettable time with his close friends. Although Moisés normally had very little alcohol, he decided that on this holiday he would make an exception, and on more than one night he drank with his friends until dawn's light crept into the sky. December twentieth arrived and Moisés's holiday came to an end. He knew that Federico would be making preparations for his grand New Year's Eve bash, a long standing tradition at his home. According to the older employees, every December thirty first, Federico hired an orchestra and invited all of his friends to ring in the New Year together. The night of the big celebration, Moisés attended Federico's party, not as a bodyguard, but as a special guest. It was an extravagant party. Moisés was feeling very happy; not because of the succulent dishes that were served, nor the ample whisky, which incidentally was beginning to go to his head, but because of Jessica. She was by his side and he was in love. They had a wonderful New Years, dancing into the wee hours and getting to know each other more deeply. When they took breaks from dancing, they talked about their private lives. As the hours passed and the alcohol took more effect on them, they divulged their most intimate secrets to each other. Moisés found out that Jessica was living in an apartment with her brother Robert, a DAS agent. Knowing how dangerous his profession was, she was always worried and anxious that something terrible would happen to him. Now, with a bodyguard as her new boyfriend, she knew that her anguish would double. With the rampant violence that besieged their country, their lives would always be at risk of death: a violent death.

Days after Federico's celebration, Moisés's job had become more relaxed. Since the criminals who had been harassing Federico had been captured and detained, the tension had eased and there were fewer red alerts with regards to Federico's security. Therefore, Moisés had more time to spend with Jessica. An immense love united them and it grew each day. They built an impenetrable fortress of love in their souls for each other. They never imagined that, with the endless possibilities that their future held, their love and dream of being together could be destroyed by dark forces.

Immersed in an illusion of endless love and happiness ahead of them, Jessica couldn't wait for Moisés to meet her brother. She suggested that he accompany her to the DAS offices where her brother worked. Next morning, Jessica introduced Moisés to agent Robert Suarez and told her brother all about Moisés and his work as Federico's bodyguard. She also made sure that her brother knew of Moisés's intentions to give up the profession the day they decided to marry.

However, Jessica was unaware of the big surprise awaiting her on that particular afternoon. Moisés had decided it was the moment to propose to her. In the middle of their conversation, Moisés took a folder from his backpack. "Robert," he said, "I would like you to check my resume and let me know if I have a chance to become a DAS agent." Robert took the folder and opened it. When he read the first words and saw the ring on the supposed file, he understood Moisés's intention. "Sorry Moisés," he said immediately with a gleam in his eye, "but people with your criminal record would never be accepted". Surprised by her brother's words, Jessica grabbed the file from her brother's hands. When she read the sentences and saw the ring she put her hands on her face, and gasped: "!Oh dios mío!" Moisés went down on one knee:

"I love you Jessica", said Moisés. "Today I need to ask you something very important! Will you marry me?"

Jessica was beaming. "You're the love of my life, and my answer is, yes, yes. Yes!" she answered ecstatically. So there, in her brother's office, the couple agreed on the marriage date and who would be the maid of honor and the best man at their wedding.

Two months before the wedding date, Moisés talked to Señor Federico about his decision. Federico congratulated him very cordially, but when Moisés announced that he would be leaving his job as personal bodyguard, his expression became serious.

"Why can't you carry on with this job after marriage?" he inquired.

Without hesitation Moisés replied that he had to keep his promise to Jessica. Federico wasn't very happy with his response, but seconds later, he realized that with Moisés's desire is to have a family, it would be irresponsible to put his life in great danger. So, very sensibly, Federico shook his hand and as proof of his gratitude for the work Moisés had done, gave him a new job as manager in one of his most profitable stores. In addition, as a wedding gift, Federico decided to cover the cost of the wedding and honeymoon. According to the Federico, this act of generosity was nothing in comparison to what Moisés had done for him.

A few days before the wedding, Jessica gave out invitations to each of her friends and Moisés invited the people closest to his heart, with a special invitation for Rocio and Joel, who would be the couple's best man and maid of honor. Their ceremony was kept simple and held in a small church. Only Federico, his wife, Moisés's fellow bodyguards, their godparents and the couple's best friends attended. Among them was Robert, Moisés's brother-in-law, who came with his girlfriend, and would walk Jessica down the aisle. Two little boys carried Jessica's pristine wedding dress train as she walked down the aisle. Dirseur, Rocio's son, was the guest of honor and the ring bearer. Once the couple had said their vows, they all left the church in two limousines and travelled to the ballroom at Arizona's hotel for the big celebration. There they enjoyed a beautiful meal, drinks while a band played rumba until the early hours of June 27th, 1986. Even when the band stopped playing at five in the morning, the festivities continued until the guests saw the newly married couple off on the airplane that would take them to Margarita Island.

After a week of bliss, Moisés and Jessica returned from their honeymoon, and Moisés began his new job as manager. However, a new surprise would await the newlyweds. That day, Federico gave them keys to an apartment as an additional wedding gift. The brand new apartment was located on the third floor of a residential complex. They were all completely unaware that a police Colonel, a "SIJIN" chief[1], lived in an apartment in the front of that same complex and at that very moment, a drug cartel was planning an attack on him. They had placed a bomb in a truck that would park directly in front of his apartment, ready to explode the moment he arrived. So with that ominous event in motion, destiny began to forge a new plot against the people that Moisés loved most. On this occasion it would act against Jessica, the woman he had married only weeks earlier.

On the fatal late afternoon when the Colonel arrived home, the criminals detonated three hundred kilos of ammonia dynamite. The blast smashed all the windows and sent splinters of glass and small metal pieces in all directions reaching Jessica, who at that moment was gazing out onto the hills from her balcony, enjoying the warm afternoon sun. The fragments penetrated her body and cut into her veins. Blood spouted uncontrollably from her wounds and a few seconds later, she died.

Even after many years, this tragic event would continue to haunt Moisés. The trauma of losing Jessica so suddenly and violently would cause a searing pain in Moisés's soul. Moisés remembered his brother-in-law Robert weeping in the cemetery on the day of the funeral, an image which only deepened his sadness and melancholy. They had both been robbed of Jessica, a woman that each of them loved in

---

1   SIJIN stands for: Servicio de inteligencia judicial contra el narcotráfico. It is a sector of the military police in charge of eliminating the drug cartels in Colombia.

their own way. It was as if their hearts had been shattered into a thousand pieces. But this tragedy that had cast a long shadow over Moisés would only be the beginning of a chain of fatalities.

In the midst of a depression that he had sunken into after losing his beloved wife, Moisés boarded a bus, travelling listlessly until it reached the end of its route. Then, he would take another bus indifferent to its destination only aching for distance; "he had become like a boat without a coxswain. One day he woke up as the bus halted and realized that he had arrived in some forlorn town of Antioquia, a province he had never travelled to. Feeling disoriented and without knowing a soul, he opted to search for a place to spend the night. His eyes were swollen and he was exhausted from his grief. He knew that all he could do was find a bed in which to sleep. In the motel room, on the bed and almost asleep, Moisés heard a commercial on TV, which he had turned on in order to break up the silence. It happened to be showing a commercial for a martial arts academy. Watching the screen, he recognized that the instructor was his friend Charles, and he scribbled down the address of the academy in San Carlos. The next morning, feeling a little better, he decided to take the bus there. Charles was very happy to see him and gave him a hug:

"Moisés!" Do you want to come over to my place?" he asked.

"Of course!", Moisés answered.

Once they arrived at Charles's home, Moisés was introduced to his grandmother Angela. She affectionately greeted Moisés and invited him to have lunch with them. Once seated at the table, Charles asked him with concern in his eyes:

"Moisés, how are things?"

Filled with melancholy, Moisés recounted his experiences in the army, his late mother's death, his days as a bodyguard and the recent tragic death of his wife Jessica. Very distressed by his losses, Charles and his grandmother both hugged him and offered words of comfort and encouragement, telling them that his life would turn for the better. Charles then told him about his life as a martial arts instructor and his most recent achievements. After finishing lunch, Charles's family invited him to spend a few days at their farm and Moisés agreed; he was desperate to forget his pain. When they arrived, he was amazed by the beautiful landscape and the friendly people. So a week later when his friends decided to leave the farm, Moisés had no desire to leave.

"Charles," he asked, "Would it be alright if I stayed at the farm for a few more days?"

"Sure! You can stay as long as you want." Charles replied. "And what's more, I'll speak with the man in charge of the farm when we're away and tell him to give you whatever you need."

At the farm, life would take another course for Moisés. He was spending his completing various chores on the farm, and although his emotional wounds were still raw, he felt he was finding the strength to move on with his life. He was learning all about life on a small cattle farm and about the transportation of milk that was sold to various dairy companies. Optimistically, he always searched for a solution to problems or injustices that arose. He didn't like that the companies were taking advantage of the circumstances and buying the milk from the local farmers at very low prices. Moisés decided to use a tractor from the farm and purchase milk from the surrounding farmers. He would pay a fair price for the milk in winter and summer. Because of this initiative, other farmers in search of a better alternative began selling their milk to him. Moisés began with buying milk produced by cattle but then had the idea to also sell veterinary and agricultural products. In a couple of months, his business was booming and Moisés became a large scale producer. Soon the garage where Moisés stocked the milk containers became too small. Moisés had not only found success in his business, but also in his personal life. He had gotten to know each of the local farmers like the fingers on his hands, farmers whose families had first settled on this land.

Only eight months after his arrival, life in the village had greatly improved due to his initiative and Moisés was determined to improve things even more. So, one afternoon, after doing some accounting and seeking new strategies, he showed the farmers that they could earn far more than they did presently. He decided to hold a meeting with everyone from the surrounding farms. At the meeting, Moisés proposed that they build a dairy factory together that would sell cheese and other milk products. Everyone liked the idea immediately and they decided to go ahead with Moisés's plan. After their agreement, they discussed the finances of the business and debated how they would raise enough money together.

Night arrived and they had created a cooperative, where everyone would put in their share and work together. However, days later, when the machines had been installed, they met their first obstacle; the room was too small for their stock and they needed a larger space. It was at that moment when Moisés met Martha, the owner of the adjoining property, who had been invited to the meeting. She was one of the largest cattle ranchers in that region and logically had no need to join the cooperative. However, she optimistically joined right away and gave them a huge storage space where they could also put the factory office. Martha's offer was a surprise to all of them. However, no one would object to her unexpected and generous offer. They understood that Martha had a reason to join them, and this reason would turn out to be Moisés.

After completing the factory installation, Moisés engaged in a pleasant conversation with the partners. They admired Martha's gesture of generosity since she had no need to become part of the cooperative. Having been widowed very young and living in the company of Christopher her adoptive son, she was considered an enigmatic woman. Since her husband's death, she supposedly hadn't become romantically involved with anyone, but this wasn't due to a lack of suitors. She turned them away one by one, robbing each of them of their hopes to be with her. One of these men was Ulises, the man in charge of the workers on the farm. He hung on to the belief that someday she would succumb to his supplications and win her heart. But she didn't pay any attention to him, and little by little a deep resentment began to grow inside him. Moisés's other partners commented that Martha's late husband had been involved in cocaine trafficking, which was how he supposedly acquired his large fortune. According to envious tongues, he had betrayed a group of narco-traffickers, which was the reason why in retaliation, the mafia had killed him and disposed of his body.

Completely focused on the business, Moisés paid no attention to Martha's past. The factory soon started their operation, producing eighty milk containers daily; these were transformed into butter and a variety of cheeses, which were distributed to shops and supermarkets in the city. While this was happening, Moisés noticed that Martha was showing interest in him. At night when he was resting, she would always find a pretext to call him in order to talk about the company's future. She would also visit him in the evenings, which made Ulises very jealous.

Months passed and the factory's production increased. In order to keep up with demand, the cooperative began buying milk from farms of adjoining regions in addition to that of the partners in the cooperative. That achievement was worth admiring. Without Moisés imagining it, one afternoon Martha came to visit Moisés and unexpectedly kissed him passionately on the lips, exclaiming that they should celebrate the factory's success. Then she invited him to dinner at one of the restaurants in the city, about thirty minutes from the farm. Moisés clearly understood her romantic intentions and although he accepted her invitation, he knew he had no choice but to clarify his feelings to her. That night, in the middle of dinner, Moisés told her that she was very beautiful and would make the man who won her heart very happy, but that he couldn't be that man. His life, he lamented, had been destined for misfortune and hurt all those he loved most. He explained that all the people closest to his heart had suffered tragedies. The ominous cloud of his destiny had been pursuing him without mercy since the day he was born, when his difficult birth almost ended his mother's life. His uncle Antonio would be massacred when he was a young boy and one of these bullets would stay lodged in his mother's body unknowingly causing her illness years later, which would be diagnosed only after her death. His beloved teacher Teresa would leave town and years later, him and his girlfriend would be separated indefinitely. Not long afterward, his friend José would die in a fire and Rocio would become mentally ill. Then there was Joel's accident and the suicide of his "buddy" Carrillo. But what had been most painful was his mother's eventual death. Once he had finally recovered from that tragedy, his wife Jessica would be his destiny's next victim when she died violently from a terrorist attack. With all these calamities, he could only conclude that it would be best for her to stay away from him.

After rapidly recounting the string of tragedies that had besieged all those he loved most, Moisés said that it was best not to get involved with him. He didn't want to bring misfortune to her life as well. He confessed that although he may appear to be disinterested, he had been thinking about her a lot lately and that he was resisting falling in love with her. Moisés lamented that it would be best to remain friends but that there was no reason why they couldn't spend time together and have fun in their spare time. After pondering Moisés's words, Martha agreed to respect his wishes.

Time took its usual course in the village and one afternoon, la señora Angela, Bridget and Charles came to the farm. They were amazed at how the community had been transformed and were even more impressed with the new cheese factory.

Moisés was happy with their presence, and greeted them with a smile as they embraced him.

"Moisés!" exclaimed la Señora Angela, "You have an impressive amount of charisma and aptitude for business in order to have such a successful factory. You should consider going into politics. It would be very good for you." Moisés humbly told her that everything he had learned was thanks to her deceased son and his great friend José. After expressing these words of appreciation while sitting at the table, they continued with their conversation. Angela told Moisés that her family didn't understand why he never came to visit them at the village, and it seemed ungrateful of him after they had given him the opportunity to stay at the farm. "It's not because I'm ungrateful that I haven't come to visit your family" responded Moisés a little distressed. "It's because I've been completely overwhelmed by my obligations. I've been working full time, seven days a week without a break. I promise to visit all of you very soon" he said. La Señora Angela looked at him with concern: "Moisés, Joel and Rocio are very worried about you because they haven't heard any news from you. This morning a few minutes before leaving, they called us at home and wanted to know if we knew where you were" said la Señora Angela.

"What did you tell them?" Moisés asked, upset with the news.

Charles replied that he only gave them his telephone number at the farm so they could reach him directly. Immediately,

Moisés ran into the house with the intention to call them. However, the moment he stepped into the living room, the phone rang and when he answered, it was Rocio.

"Moisés! What a relief that you're okay," she said breathlessly. "We were worried sick about you because we hadn't heard from you since Jessica's funeral. We looked for you in Cucuta and placed ads in the newspaper and radio, but it was impossible to find you. Nobody knew where you were. Robert, your brother-in-law, reported you as missing. He sent several colleagues faxes with your photograph and personal information from his DAS office, so that they could search for you in other cities, but when months passed without locating you, he lost hope of ever finding you alive. Señor Federico decided to hire a private detective, who is still looking for you. Federico was so worried that he called me to find out if we knew anything".

After hearing the worry and pain that he had caused his friends, Moisés felt terrible. He was grateful, however, to all of his friends for being so concerned and for going to such lengths to find him. Then he told Rocio that he was living at Charles's farm close to the town of Antioquia. He said that the time he had spent on the farm had helped him significantly and he had managed to control his depression brought on by Jessica's death. For the first time in many months, he added, he even felt like he could be happy again. Before ending the conversation he promised Rocio that they would see each other soon. He said his good byes and told them to give his godson Dirseur a hug from him. A few seconds after hanging up, Moisés decided to call Robert and then Federico to let them know he was alright.

THE CREATION OF SELF-DEFENSE OF THE GROUP OF FARMERS

Moisés remembered the moment when unsettling news reached the farmers, the kind of news that was not uncommon in those days. A very well-organized criminal band was in the region, which produced fear and deep concern among the landowners. The farmers heard daily rumors that the criminals had infiltrated farms located on the north side. They had already robbed cattle from several properties and killed some administrators in the lower part of the village as a way to supress any possible resistance. Martha was one of the farmers most concerned with this rumor. She was consumed by fear and one afternoon came looking for Moisés.

"Moisés!" She exclaimed. "What should we do if the criminals attack us?"

Moisés answered her calmly; "First we should not panic", he said. "Second, we should organize a meeting with all the landowners in the northern region and together we can devise a strategy to defend our property."

Not long afterward, Martha had organized the meeting. All the farmers had the opportunity to express their opinion during the gathering. Moisés designed a plan of defense, and explained to the farmers that the most vulnerable farms would be protected by an alarm system. The alarms would be heard instantly in all the surrounding properties when they were being attacked. Everyone agreed with his plan and that same day they bought the materials they would need. After the alarms were installed, there were some additional details that needed to be discussed. Moisés knew that all the farmers were experienced with handling weapons, but he needed to teach them combat tactics so that they knew how to act in the moment of an attack. This would be of utmost importance since the criminals operated at night. The first of these tactics would be that the farmers would defend themselves by wearing white T-shirts. So, in case of a criminal attack, there would be no confusion as to who their enemy was.

The second point that they agreed on was not to use any kind of motor vehicles during a criminal attack, only cavalry. In addition, Moisés clarified that their advance would be in small groups, and on foot within one hundred meters of the farm that was being attacked. The third point he emphasized was that they should shoot to injure the criminals, not kill them. The band members wouldn't abandon wounded band members, but rather attempt to carry them to safety. According to Moisés, this would be an advantage for the farmers since it would give them a chance to identify the criminals. Moisés also decided that the village entrance and exit should be left free of men. Furthermore, since there were thirty-six farmers, four would enter the property they were defending and cause a stampede of cattle where the criminals were gathered. The rest of the farmers would position themselves tactically and wait for Moises's signal of "two shots to the air", to begin their assault. That plan was repeated several times so that in the moment of a counter-attack, everything would go smoothly.

At this point in telling the story, Moisés paused. He took a deep breath, and then recalled an evening when at precisely seven twenty five, the alarm rang and fifteen minutes later all the farm owners had gathered except for Martha and Ulises, the foreman, who according to Moisés, had been watching Martha's property. During the criminal attack, the six groups under Moises's command proceeded with their plan. Ten minutes after meeting together on horseback they all dismounted and began on foot toward "The new horizon farm", Gustavo's Fuente's property.

In groups of six, everyone took their position. Moisés, who was chosen to cause the stampede of cattle, very cautiously approached the house while Carmelo and Christopher covered his back. So when Moisés first entered the building, he could see through the window that the criminals had tied up the foreman and his family. He also observed belongings that had been thrown onto the floor by other bandits, who evidently had been searching for money and items of value. Moisés also noted that in the cow-shed, the robbers had gathered almost 80 cattle to be led out of the property. Moisés very carefully approached them, opened the cow-shed gate. He fired two shots from his shotgun into the air. This caused a stampede, and at the same time the offenders tried to find the person who had challenged them. But the bandits did not know that a surprise awaited them outside. So when they ran out, they were fired from all sides. The bandits were powerless and unprepared for the attack and opted to withdraw. Moisés and his group, keeping a safe distance, pursued them for about one hundred meters down towards the village. At this point dawn's light began to illuminate the landscape and Moisés and the other men abandoned their pursuit not wanting to be recognized by the outlaws.

The confrontation between the bandits and Moisés's group had come to an end on Gustavo's property. However, Martha's progressive farm, as she called it, once a place of tranquility was taut with tension. Besides a new fear that had seeped into the air of the region, her foreman, Ulises began to voice his discontentment and resentment. Pained by her continual rejections, he felt sick to his stomach when he witnessed the affection she so easily showed Moisés. He couldn't contain himself any longer.

"Martha!" Ulises said, his voice thick with hurt and anger. "Why is it that in all the time you've been on your own you've never paid any attention to me, knowing that I'm in love with you? How is it possible that you can love a stranger who you've only met months ago?

Martha felt outraged by the foreman's bad behavior. "Ulises!" she said exasperated, "Love comes from the heart and Moisés is the one who managed to take love by the reins and win my heart." Ulises was devastated by her words, his pride deeply wounded. "Martha", he said, his pain instantly turning into hatred. "This doesn't end here. You have betrayed me and you'll pay dearly". Ulises then strode furiously out of the house, slamming the door behind him.

Hours after the heated argument, Moisés and his men came back to Martha's farm. Martha was amazed when she heard that everything had gone so well. She joyfully embraced them and gave them each a shot of brandy. Then she took Moisés by the hand and together they walked to the kitchen. Once they had sat down at the table she confided in him about the confrontation she had had with Ulises. "Martha, don't worry about him" said Moisés. "I am sure that Ulises is just jealous". Moisés listened to Martha about what had occurred in more detail during his absence, then, the two returned to the main room. When the farmers of the association saw them, they got up, ready to leave and return to their farms. Before leaving, Moisés recommended that they be even more vigilant than before. He thought that they should take additional safety measures and expand the network of alarms; he was sure the bandits wouldn't retreat and would retaliate at any time.

Two days later, Moisés was surprised by the noise of several cars approaching the farm. He had no idea that Ulises's threat to Martha would be transformed into action. Suspecting that it was the criminal band, Moisés retrieved his shotgun and climbed to the top of the hill. From there he could see that the cars were the police. Breathing a sigh of relief, Moisés tucked the gun into his coat pocket and went over to welcome them. Upon their arrival, not yet spotting Moisés, the police first spoke to Señor Carmelo, one of the farm workers. "We are the National Police and we are looking for Señor Moisés Fernandez!" the sergeant exclaimed. As they didn›t hear an immediate response, the sergeant repeated the phrase again. Moisés, who was waiting on the other side, approached them and confirmed, "I am the person you're looking for. How can I help you?"

The Sergeant, who was in charge of the commission, pointed his weapon at him. "You are under arrest!" he said curtly. Moisés was taken aback.

"Under what charge?" he asked.

"You are being detained for forming an illegal armed group" the Sergeant responded. "We have a statement from the person who accused you. You must come with us." Then, another officer immediately locked Moisés's his wrists in a pair of handcuffs. "You have the right to remain silent and call a lawyer" he stated. The officer reminded Moisés that anything he said could be used against him.

Meanwhile, Martha, who had set off the alarm, sent Carmelo to find the farmers on the North side, while she went out to meet with members on the South side. Once together, she explained to them that they weren't meeting because of another bandit attack and let them know what was happening. The farmers put their horses and weapons away and got into their cars, which formed a long procession as they drove to the San Carlos police station. There, they were welcomed by the Commander of the station, who was a good friend of Martha's. Because of her great influence in the region, she was the one who spoke in Moisés's defense. She explained to the officer that Moisés had not acted alone, but rather, all thirty-five farmers present, including her, were guilty. She also clarified that they had organized a group in order to defend their property and the authorities should be grateful to them for their efforts because in reality this was the police's job, but they were too busy with other concerns. "Our group is not illegal as you are insinuating" she explained. "Everyone has a license for their weapons, and according to the military forces, these weapons were used to defend ourselves in a time of crisis." After Martha's statement of defense, the Commander acknowledged his mistake. Immediately, he ordered that Moisés be released. Before Moisés left the station, the officer apologized to him for the misunderstanding.

Once set free, everyone was happy except Moisés. A bad feeling lingered inside him. The town's newspaper had made him out to be the farmers' leader, which left him even more vulnerable to a future attack by the criminal band. He knew that he had no choice but to take new security measures. From that day on, he and his military group were resolute in their work to be on guard every night, all night until first dawn's light cast orange and pinks over the hills. For several consecutive weeks they watched the village entrance closely.

During the ensuing days of surveillance, Moisés found out that the complaint against him was filed by Ulises. Even so, Moisés didn't give the event much importance. However, Martha reacted differently. Martha called Ulises to her office, paid him his benefit and fired him. After that, a relative calm returned to the village, but Moisés and his men refused to lower their guard. His military group maintained itself on maximum alert.

Two months later, Moisés and his men would be surprised by a TV newscast. In a last-minute bulletin, the anchorman reported that a gang of criminals called the "The devil's angels" were killed by the army in a confrontation that took several hours. These outlaws were accused of assaulting the North of Antioquia, a rural area where their actions left death and desolation in their wake. After watching the news story, Moisés and his group understood that by the alias and way operating, "The devil angels" were the same gang of bandits who attempted to rob Gustavo Fuentes's property months earlier. The news gave the farms a huge sense of relief. With the death of these evildoers, their fear evaporated. Excited by the news, Martha looked at Moisés with joy in her eyes. "We have to celebrate!" she said. She invited him to dinner and then to a dance club. Moisés accepted the invitation without hesitation and confirmed that he would pick her up at six thirty.

That night, at last they felt like they could relax and have a good time. After a delicious dinner, they danced and consumed alcohol until three o'clock in the morning. By this time Moisés was ready to go back to the farm and told Martha that he'd like to go home. Still intoxicated, Martha told him that it was too late and dangerous to drive home. She thought it best to find a place to stay nearby until they had slept off the alcohol. Convinced, Moisés got them a hotel room nearby. In two separate beds they attempted to get some sleep. But Moisés and Martha both felt restless. He noticed her tossing and turning in the bed beside him. She stood up twice to come toward him and although he was pretending to sleep, he could see that she was only wearing a bra and tiny panties. When she was near Moises's bed, she turned around and went back to her bed. Ten minutes later she lost her ability to resist him and crawled under the blankets with Moisés. He pretended not to notice and to sleep but then she began to caress him. Moisés could not resist her erotic touch. They began to kiss and soon abandoned themselves to each other and had sex. Later that morning, neither of them resisted their desire for one another any longer.

Moisés knew that their relationship had shifted. From that moment on, they openly displayed their affection for each other and everyone would see them embracing and kissing in the village. Their love transformed their loneliness into bliss and their eyes shone with love for each other. Martha was so in love that whenever she met with friends, she would only talk about Moisés. She would confide in her friends that he was the man she had always dreamed of and the first man she truly loved. Moisés was also in love, but experience had taught him to be cautious. He was worried that destiny's misfortune would once again unveil itself on the person he loved most.

A NEW EPISODE OF DEATH

Moisés enjoyed several months of uninterrupted bliss with Martha. He even began to believe that his misfortune had come to an end. The afternoon when Moisés considered that possibility, Gustavo's friend visited Martha's farm. Upon his arrival, Moisés instantly noticed Gustavo's worried expression. His attitude made him think that something had happened to make Gustavo fearful.

"How are things, Gustavo?" Moisés asked inquisitively. "Is something worrying you?" Uncertainty was etched in Gustavo's face. "It's nothing serious" he replied with hesitation. "It's just that I was in Arcades visiting my sister and I saw guerrillas in town acting like they owned the place. What was most surprising was how Ulises, Martha's former foreman, was the leader of this subversive group. Since I know that Martha and Ulises have had more than one argument, I wanted to warn her so that he wouldn't take her by surprise." Gustavo paused, and took a breath before continuing. "I leave the decision to warn Martha in your hands. The town of Arcades is on the other side of the mountains, about 200 kilometers to the south, so the best thing to do is to remain on alert". Before leaving, Gustavo warned him to be careful because he knew that Ulises was both dangerous and treacherous. They shook hands goodbye. "If you need help" Gustavo insisted, "you can count on me anytime!" Moisés was grateful to his neighbour, thanked him and promised to heed his warning.

Once Señor Gustavo had left, Martha came into the room, unaware of what had transpired. "Honey, you seem so worried", she said looking at him intently. "What were you two talking about?" Moisés didn't want to worry her. "We were talking about the cattle problem" he lied. He told me that the milk production was declining. He also asked me what measures should be taken to make up for the deficit. This decline is a problem since it will affect our cheese production!" he added. Moisés's lie did have some truth to it. Milk production had declined recently.

The news Gustavo revealed to Moisés didn't frighten him nor did the problem with the milk production. He had a solution in mind for both. Moisés was optimistic. That same afternoon, he came up with several possible solutions to the cattle problem that he suggested to Martha in order for her to decide the most viable option. "Even though I'm the owner of the farm", she said assuredly, "I have complete faith in whatever you decide to do."

Moisés first worked on finding a solution to the coming milk crisis. He met with Martha's farm workers and told them to remove all the cows that had an average age of seven. The second step was to find a customer who would buy the cattle. The third aspect of the dilemma concerned cheese production. To maintain it, they would have to buy milk from farms in other municipalities in order to make up their shortage. After making these decisions, Moisés called a meeting with the members of the Cooperative and suggested that they do the same with their cattle. Without thinking twice, they followed his example.

Hours later, Martha's farm labour had gathered a total of two hundred and thirty-six cattle to be sold that same day. With the money from the sale, Moisés bought two hundred and six Swiss calves and twenty-seven new bulls that were of the Buffalo breed. They would be doing the work of a stallion.

According to Moisés, the breed combination between the Buffalo and Swiss, would produce calves that were much more productive in the short term.

That afternoon, the new calves that had arrived raised the total number of cattle on the property, which would unfortunately mean that they risked being harassed even more by illegal groups. So as a safety measure, Moisés recommended that Martha have houses built on the property for the workers whom had been with her longest. In addition, he would provide each of them with a licensed weapon so that they could work while also providing security to the ranch. Martha agreed to Moisés's idea and he immediately began to work on the project.

Once the new farm houses had been constructed, it was time for a vacation. So, Moisés proposed to Martha that they take a trip together to visit his friends, Rocio, Joel and his godson Dirseur. He had promised to visit them a long time ago and it was time that he saw them. Martha was excited by the invitation:

"That's a great idea!" she exclaimed. "But who can we leave in charge of the ranch?"

Moisés immediately thought of Christopher. He was a young veterinarian that Martha loved like a son. He was one of the worker's sons, and since his mother's death, he had lived on the farm. Christopher was easy going and had won the confidence and appreciation of everyone who knew him. As a reward for his good behavior, Martha had insisted that he finish high school and after paid for his tuition at University. Christopher was very grateful to her and treated her with love and loyalty. After he obtained his veterinarian degree, Christopher had become responsible for the cattle on Martha's farm.

Not long afterward Christopher came to the house to congratulate Moisés on his idea to sell the older cows and breed new Swiss calves with the Buffalo breed.

"Christopher," Moisés said, "we made a decision without first talking to you. We decided that you could manage the farm for a few days while we go on a short vacation."

"Thanks, I'd love to", answered Christopher feeling honored. "I feel honored that you thought of me. You know I would do anything to help you."

The day before leaving Martha's farm, Moisés reminded Christopher how to maintain safety on the farm and activate the alarm system. Then Moisés invited him to a meeting with Martha's workers and the members of the cooperative, at which time he explained to everyone that he and Martha would be away for a few days. He reminded them how to respond in the case of any attack. He also reminded the workers that in case they need to defend the farm, it would be necessary to coordinate their efforts with the other members of the cooperative. During their absence Moisés would be in contact with them by telephone.

The couple went to the airport and from there took a flight to the Ocaña where they would continue their journey by taxi to Convención, Moisés's town. It just so happened that they arrived shortly before the Sugar festival. So before visiting Joel and Rocio, they toured the town. Its main streets were decorated with streamers and everyone was jubilant with anticipation of the festivities. The air was fragrant with the aroma of honey and coffee coming from farms with mills and grinding machines; these products were the town's two main industries. That evening, Moisés met several of his friends while they sauntered through town. After greeting him with a hug, he proudly introduced his girlfriend to them. Moisés showed Martha the parish, El Monte de Carmelo, the church, San José and "El doce de enero", the neighbourhood where

Moisés grew up. He also brought her to Jesús Conde, a parcel of land that Moisés had fled to often when life was difficult. He told her that he would come here to think when those he loved most had died. From an early age, however, he knew he would never find an answer to why these tragedies had occurred even though he still searched for a reason. Last but not least, Moisés showed Martha the «Tun Tun», the creek where he and his friends always went to swim and cool off.

After the tour, Moisés asked the taxi driver to take them to El Hotel de María. They were lucky because when they arrived there was only one vacant room available. The next day after breakfast, they went into town to buy a gift for Moisés's godson, since they had forgotten his gift on the airplane. To find the same gift in the town's stores was impossible. The only store where they could find it was at Mariela's miscellanea, but Moisés wanted to surprise his friends and decided not to go there. So after thinking about another gift, they opted to buy him roller skates. It was the new rage and they were being sold in all the stores. Martha put Diseur's roller skates in her suitcase so they wouldn't get lost. Now they were ready to surprise their friends.

When they arrived, the store was teaming with customers. While Joel and three employees were attending them, he spotted Moisés out of the corner of his eye. A big smile spread across his face. Moisés went over to him and gave him a big hug and then introduced him to Martha. Then Moisés asked Joel about Rocio and he said that she was in the backyard with Diseur. Joel was excited to see Moisés alive. "Moisés! Where have you been, what's been going on in your life?" he asked. "We were very worried because we hadn't heard from you in several months".

"Forgive me Joel", Moisés answered a little ashamed, "but I was so distraught that I was living like a hermit and need to be alone with Jessica's memory".

After his apology, Moisés walked into the backyard to look for Rocio, who was having fun playing with her son. She didn't notice him as he approached her quietly, and he decided he would surprise her. From behind he put his hands over the Rocio's eyes. Startled and confused she started to guess who it could be. Suddenly Rocio's hand touched Moses's arm and she felt one of his scars. "Moisés!" "Moisés!" she cried. She turned around and hugged him. Then she took Diseur's hand and affectionately told him. "Bebé get out of the bathtub and greet your Godfather". Moisés happily embraced them with his arms and said:

"Today you will meet someone who is very special to me".

They walked from the patio to the warehouse. When Martha saw them, she got up from the chair and went to meet them. "Honey!" Moisés said. "This is Rocio, the friend who I always talkabout, and this is Diseur my godson". Martha greeted them warmly and kissed them on the cheek. She smiled.

"It's a pleasure to finally meet Moisés's dearest friends", said Martha. Then she started playing with Diseur. At that moment Moisés noticed how much happiness a child would bring to Martha's life. Joel unintentionally interrupted the moment, and shouted joyfully: "We have to celebrate!" He uncorked a bottle of wine, and together they made a toast to their friendship.

With the expression of surprise still etched in her face, Rocio told Moisés that they had been searching for him all over and had asked people in the town's churches to pray for his well-being. "Although many thought that you were dead", she said her voice filling with emotion, "all of us kept hoping to see you alive." After hearing the grief that his silence had caused, Moisés apologized to them again. He attempted to explain to them that the tragic events of loss and then Jessica's violent death had made him want to disappear. He would walk aimlessly without any idea where he was going. Confused, he traveled from one place to another guided only by his instinct to survive. He had even suffered some amnesia; his senses were entirely consumed by his longing for Jessica. As Moisés talked the hours passed and when he paused to look up, he saw on that the hands on the clock on the wall pointed to seven thirty. At that moment, Joel invited them to «El Paisa» a restaurant they hastily called to make a reservation for dinner. They would go just the four of them and leave Diseur with his grandmother. At the restaurant they enjoyed a succulent meal accompanied by pleasant conversation and wine.

When the church bell rang, announcing the arrival of midnight, the restaurant and bar closed and the couples got up to leave. Moisés and Martha began walking towards their hotel and they stopped to say goodbye to Joel and Rocio.

"You aren't thinking of staying at a hotel tonight are you?" asked Rocio, surprised.

"We already paid for two nights at the hotel and have all of our things there" answered Moisés, feeling a little embarrassed. "Okay Moisés! But tomorrow you and Martha better stay with us" Joel objected. "We will have a nice room ready for you".

The next day after breakfast, the couple walked through town on their way to Rocio's house. There was a band dressed in brightly coloured costumes playing merengue on the street corner ready to throw water and cornstarch on the crowd of onlookers. They were waiting for noon when the ringing of the church bells would mark the beginning of the Carnival.

When Martha and Moisés reached Joel's neighbourhood, they met his friends who had joined the rumba. Each profession in town had their own "fiesta" or "rumba" as part of the festivities of the Carnival. The Merengue group that enlivened this party was made up of drivers. After greeting his friends and having few beer, they left the drivers' party and walked for several blocks. After meeting up with Joel and Rocio, they watched the parade of women who were competing to become "La reina del pueblo" or the beauty queen of the town. Joel was enjoying himself so much that he completely forgot that they were supposed to be at the business club. Rocio reminded him of the invitation.

After spending some time at the club, the four of them went to La plaza de los prisioneros, a nice park where they continued enjoying the festivities. They were splashed with water, carnival talc there and even paint. Covered in paint, the four then headed to the main square where there was a big crowd. They had come to hear the famous Colombian singer, Alfredo Gutierrez, who would be preforming that night. They were on the south side of the stage where they found the only two empty tables. What they didn't know was the reason these tables weren't occupied. People were trying to avoid Maximiliano, a man conversing with his friends, close by. People in town were afraid of him, not only because he was a massive guy, but because he had a well-deserved reputation for picking fights. He had sometimes caused brawls and anything could set him off. He believed he was the best fighter in the region, and was more than eager to test out his skills.

When Joel was getting up from the table he mistakenly tipped over his cup of beer, which spilled onto Maximiliano's legs. The man stood up angrily, ready to hit Joel but his friends managed to restrain him. Joel cautiously apologized to him, assuring him that it was an accident. Maximiliano didn't accept Joel's apology. Beginning to feel worried, Moisés felt he should intervene. He rose from the chair, bought four cups of beer and put them on Maximiliano's table to try and amend the situation. Maximilian took Moises's gesture as an offense and began insulting him. Moisés pretended not to hear him, but Maximiliano continued.

A few hours later, Moisés rose from his chair with the intention of using the bathroom that was at the far side of the plaza. As he was walking, he suddenly realized that he was surrounded. It was Maximiliano and his friends. The people who knew Maximiliano were prepared to see an unequal fight. Many of them cautiously approached them. Some teenage boys who had heard the argument between them and knew both of them wanted them to fight.

"Fight!, !Fight!" They chanted. "Maximiliano and Moisés are going to fight!," some shouted. When the shouting reached Martha's ears, she rose like a feline to defend Moisés, but Joel took her by the arm.

"Calm down" he urged her. "Moisés can deal with them". Martha pulled away from him and rushed towards the place where the events were taking place. When she arrived, the fight was seconds from beginning. Furious, Maximiliano threw the first punch at Moisés, but he dodged it and with his right arm punched Maximiliano in the stomach, knocking the wind out of him. Maximiliano hunched over in pain. Immediately, Moisés followed this hit with the kung Fu "ax hit", which knocked his feet from under him and he slammed facedown to the ground. However, because of Maximiliano's strength he managed to stagger up. With a wicked smirk, he then pulled a knife out of his pocket. With the knife in hand, he tried to stab Moisés. But Moisés swiftly grabbed his arm, stopping it in mid-air. At the same time and with great speed he twisted Maximiliano's forearm. This maneuver made Maximiliano scream out in pain and forced him to drop the weapon. When one of Maximiliano's friends saw that Moisés was winning the fight, he tried to attack him from behind. But he would also be surprised by Moisés, who with a flying kick straight to the chin knocked the man unconscious.

It was precisely at that moment that the police arrived and arrested them. They charge them for causing a public scandal.

At the police station, with broken teeth and a bleeding nose, Maximiliano and his friend charged Moisés. The police commander ordered the three guys be detained in a cell. However, when Moisés explained how the fight had been instigated, they decided to lift the charges against him and he was free to leave. "It's the first time that they have lost fight!", the commander said with admiration." Usually they're here for beating someone to a pulp and this time they're the ones complaining for being beaten".

After, the police officer said: "Señor Moisés, it's up to you if we detain Maximiliano and his friends for seventy-two hours or if we drop the charges and let them go". Moisés thought for a moment. "I think they've learned their lesson so I won't press charges and you can free them whenever you find it convenient", Moisés replied.

After the fight, people from the town gained a new respect for Moisés since he had been the only one to put Maximiliano and his friends in their place. From then on, those who had been terrorized by Maximilian or believed him to be an unstoppable bully, no longer saw him as a threat. Once Moisés had returned to their friend's home from the police station, Martha embraced him.

"Cariño," she exclaimed, both with relief and admiration. "I had no idea you were an expert fighter".

A few seconds later, Rocio and Joel expressed how proud they were of him: "Well-done Moisés; you finally knocked Maximiliano off his pedestal." Moisés was slightly annoyed by the comment. His only motive had been to defend himself and he was anxious to get off the topic. "Let's not dwell on what happened and get back to the party", he said. So they switched topics and decided to enjoy the festivities that continued to the break of dawn.

When orange and red fingers of light spread into the night sky the four exhausted friends walked to Joel's place to sleep.

Moisés slept soundly until ten-thirty in the morning. When he woke up, Martha and Rocio were already in the kitchen preparing catfish broth. This recipe, according to them, could raise the dead! In the meantime Joel had gone out to buy a few drinks in order to prepare his special concoction for hangovers. When Joel came back, he arrived with his mother and Diseur. When the child saw Moisés he launched himself off the couch into his arms and started to play fight with him. Later on, they all gathered together in the dining room to eat the delicious broth. They decided to go to the cemetery that afternoon to visit Mariela's grave. A wave of nostalgia swept over Rocio. "Since Mariela's death, we have visited her tomb every Monday" she said. "We always place fresh flowers on her grave and say a prayer".

After praying, Moisés and Martha headed back to the hotel to shower and change. Once they had returned to Joel's house, Martha recommended that they contact Christopher. Moisés took her advice and called him immediately from the hotel's reception. Moisés greeted him. "Christopher, how are things there?" he asked.

"The usual", he answered casually. "There's nothing to worry about. Enjoy your vacation and if anything happens, I'll know what to do." Both Moisés and Martha were relieved to hear that all was well on the farm. They left the hotel feeling relaxed. They were on way to a bull fight. They would meet their friends half way there and walk together.

Before arriving to the town square, two children came up to them, stopping them in their tracks. One of them approached Moisés and asked with admiration in his eyes cried out:

"Señor!" "Señor! Is it true that you're the one who knocked out Maximiliano?" Moisés smiled.

"Yes! bebé, but I was just defending myself because the guy attacked me" he replied. "Did you hear him?" said the boy looking over at his friend. "So I win the bet and you have to give me five pesos" he said nudging his friend.

The children's bet reflected the sentiment of doubt among some people that Moisés had really been capable of defending himself against Maximiliano. After the bull fight, they looked for a place to continue enjoying the festival, but because all the tables were full, they stopped on the street to ask a Merengue band to play for them. They paid them a fee and listened to them until nightfall. Then they decided to go to "Fruta tropicana», a discoteque with a live band. They danced all night. When they became tired, they planned a trip to "El Río Candado" the following day.

So with the arrival of the new day, Rocio and Joel invited their closest friends and family to go to the river. At the river, they swam, sang and told jokes. Martha was the happiest of all of them, and played with Diseur the whole time. Seeing Martha with Diseur, reminded Moisés of his own childhood when he used to accompany his mother on the long trips to the river. Mariela would often interrupt her work washing clothing to play with him. These moment were special to him filled with relaxation and happiness. As Moisés reminisced, he was interrupted by the sound of the horn coming from the van. The driver wanted to let them know that he had come back to pick them up. After finishing a short tour of the area, Moisés realized that this day together had been the best way to show gratitude to his closest friends who had prayed for him for months.

The next morning, the couple said goodbye to Rocio, Joel and Diseur, and took a taxi to Ocaña's airport, where they boarded a flight with a stopover in Medellín.

Once they were back on the farm, Martha as Moisés's energy had been restored. Their renewed energy radiated from their eyes. The time they had spent with their closest friends had soothed the body and spirit. The first person to welcome them was Christopher, who was very happy to see them. A few minutes later their arrival, the new foreman and farmworkers also came to Martha's house. After warm greetings, they gathered in the main hall. Martha was eager to know how things had gone at the farm while they were away. "Did you find anyone trespassing on our property?" she asked. They told her that everything was under their control and they hadn't seen anyone. "|Were you able to complete the new drinking pools for the animals?" she then inquired. John, who was the farm worker responsible for this task, assured her that the pools were finished and functioning. He added that the lamps placed around the new farm houses were also working. He went on to explain that they had also increased the size of the timber yard and finished branding all the new cattle. In sum, all the work had been completed ahead of schedule. In addition, as a security measure, he had installed an electric fence with wires with sensors that would warn them of any abnormal activity.

Martha was pleased with John's initiative, having installed an electric fence. However, it still needed to put up several warnings due to the high voltage between eight in the evening and four o'clock in the morning in order to ensure that no livestock could be transferred during that time period. Moisés was pleased with the new security measures taken. It would decrease the number of "cuatreros", those who would come to kill a couple cows for meat in order to sell them at the market. It would also prevent neighbour calves from coming onto Martha's pastures.

Soon it would be a year that Martha and Moisés had been living together as a couple and they would celebrate their first anniversary together. The day of their anniversary would coincide with Martha's birthday. Moisés surprised Martha with flowers and a serenade. Without realizing it, he would achieve two objectives with his gesture of love. The first would consolidate his love for Martha, while the second reminded her that he had not forgotten her birthday. Elated, she invited him and the group who had serenaded her to the living room. Moisés took her into his arms and kissed her passionately. "Darling," he said. "I hope that your life will always be full of happy moments, and that you'll never experience sadness that would bring tears to your beautiful eyes. I hope that god will bless us with many more years together." He was overcome with emotion.

"My love! Close your eyes, I have a surprise for you." He said, taking the stance of a medieval knight. He then pulled a box from his pocket, opened it and handed her an engagement ring. When she opened her eyes Moisés proposed to her in front of all the guests. Tears were streaming down Martha's cheeks as she took him by the hand. "Mi amor!" she said, her voice filled with emotion. "You have made this the happiest day of my life, I love you and my answer is yes." After embracing again, they agreed that the wedding would take the place the following month on Sunday the 27th.

That moment marked the beginning of a flurry of activity as Martha began preparations for the wedding with great anticipation. She sent out the invitations and chose her dress. The best man and the bridesmaid were chosen by mutual agreement. La señora Angela or her grandson Charles would accompany Moisés down the aisle, while Christopher would take Martha. Having decided to get married both had given free rein to their desires. And although they had sex as any normal couple, they were careful that Martha would not become pregnant before their wedding day.

The special day arrived and everything was ready. The best man and the maid of honor and bridesmaids arrived a day in advance to enjoy a party before the wedding. After the a night of fun, friends and family came together with the couple in the church, waiting for the ceremony to begin and for the bride and groom to walk down the aisle. Moisés remembered the Eucharist, and the wedding vows the priest would ask them in front of the altar. "You as a couple must be joined in marriage until death do you part" he said. And the priest would continue with Moisés repeating, "Only Martha's death could separate us and our immense love for each other".

As Moisés remembered his vows to Martha, his voice slowly trailed off. I was lost in my own thoughts so it was only after a minute of silence that I noticed it had grown quiet and I wondered if he might have left. But when I looked up, I saw that Moisés was still there and I knew, looking at him, that his silence was due to nostalgia; he had been invaded by sadness. A tear rolled down his cheek. A few minutes later, he regained his composure. He cleared his throat, wiped his eyes and continued telling his story.

He recounted the morning of the wedding when Martha walked down the aisle with Christopher, Moisés's best man. As she held onto Christopher's arm and walked toward the altar, Moisés had been awestruck by Martha's exquisite beauty. She hadn't chosen a traditional wedding gown; she was dressed in a fitted crimson skirt with a white blouse that revealed a slight neckline. Her elegant outfit was completed with black leather heels, a white hat and long delicate gloves.

As the wedding march played, soon Moisés and the bridesmaids would join the bride at the altar. Moisés soon grew impatient as he waited for the priest to finish his advice to the couple. He was jubilant when the priest finally announced: "You can kiss the bride!"

That evening, minutes after arriving at the farm, the workers who were unable to attend the ceremony at the church embraced the newlyweds and wished them luck. Then the wedding celebration began. A popular band that played salsa and merengue arrived from the capital to enliven the reception. All the members of the cooperative attended as well as the farm workers. They celebrated through the night and into the light of dawn. Moisés recalled that he and Martha had decided to postpone their honeymoon since the date was too proximate to the tragic anniversary of Jessica's death.

One evening, three months after the wedding, Martha approached Moisés. Happiness emanated from her eyes as she revealed to him that she was pregnant. Martha's happiness wasn't surprising since she had always wanted a child, and having a baby with the man she loved filled her heart with joy. Moisés was elated that he was going to be a father for the first time. He wanted to give their child all the love and tenderness that he never received from his own father.

However, as Martha's belly grew Moisés became more and more anxious. Fate reminded him that it was when he was happiest that something terrible would happen to hurt those he loved most. In order to bring some ease to his anxiety, he spoke with Martha's personal physician about his fear, and he reminded Martha to do periodic checkups to ensure that the pregnancy was progressing normally. The first seven months of Martha's pregnancy passed without any abnormal symptoms. When the day arrived and Martha went into labour, a small complication would strike fear into the hearts of Moisés and Martha. But the doctor found a solution, and a couple minutes after the emergency, their first child was born; a healthy baby boy.

Rocio, who called the couple often to find out how Martha was doing, would be the first friend to hear the good news. Rocio was elated by the arrival of the baby. From that moment on, however, Moisés's life would change dramatically. His usual relaxed state was taken over by one that put him on maximum alert; he was prepared to fight for his new family and defend them in case of adversity. In hope of preventing anything bad from happening to his son, he had him baptized when he was just a few days old. Martha didn't realize that his wish to baptize their son so soon was an attempt to undo a premonition. She agreed and at the ceremony they decided on the baby's name. He would be called Jaime.

Moisés remembered that when his son was six months old they rode through the property on horseback. From the first time Jaime would ride horseback, Moisés noticed a sparkle of joy in his eyes. When Jaime turned a year old, they threw a big birthday party with an open invitation for anyone who wanted to attend. That day Moisés, with Martha's blessing, bought their son a beautiful gift: a pony with excellent gait and all saddled up ready to ride.

With the arrival of Jaime, Moisés had everything a man could desire in his life; a woman who loved him, a son who was the light of his eyes, health, money and respect from people of the entire region. The milk production at the farms had also greatly improved. Crossing the Buffalo cattle with the other breed was producing excellent results. The cattle from the cooperative had even become self-sufficient in terms of milk production. Day by day the production was increasing and because of that, the cheese factory always had a surplus of milk which the cooperative sold to dairy companies.

In the village, the days passed peacefully. Martha was occupied with looking after Jaime, her principal entertainment, and never had time for much else. Moisés, although busy with managing the factory and with his administrative duties, never lowered his guard, wanting to ensure Martha's and Jaime are safety at all times. When Christopher helped with work, Moisés would sometimes play with Jaime all afternoon, and Martha would go out jogging to shed the extra pounds she had put on during her pregnancy. They both focused their attention on Jaime and little by little saw that he was growing up just as dew drops from the mountain become a stream and then a swift and deep river.

Once Jaime was three he had turned into a miniature cowboy; he toured the ranch on his pony and proved to be a skilled rider. He was able to maneuver his fine animal with great aptitude, which left many workers with their mouths agape with surprise. Jaimes's talent filled Moisés and Martha with pride. Although Moisés was well aware of his underlying fear, he had no idea that at that very moment destiny was forging a new plot against his happiness.

Guerrillas had just kidnapped a very influential politician and according to army intelligence services, the bandits were hiding in a camp in El alto de Lucas, the mountainous region about a hundred kilometers from Martha's farm. So when Martha and Moisés woke up a few mornings later, they saw that their property had been surrounded by the army command in charge of kidnappings. In order to rescue the politician, they had taken possession of Martha's farm and had established a mobile base camp close to Moisés's factory. From there, they coordinated their plan of attack. With a strategy called "Operación rastrillo" or "Operation rake", they would ambush the guerrillas on the mountain top with a special command that would approach stealthily from behind and take them by surprise. The rebels would then be forced to flee to the base of the mountain and undoubtedly make a counter attack. Then military troops would be deployed from Martha's property to execute "Operación herradura" or "Operation horseshoe" to ambush the second group of guerillas who came down from the mountain, all in effort to free the politician.

Back at the ranch everything went on as usual despite the disturbing presence of the army. Although everyone was nervous with their presence on the grounds, nobody imagined that by that same afternoon a tragic event would unfold. While life remained relatively calm within the boundaries of the farm, up in the mountains a dramatic showdown was taking place between the military and the rebels. The army achieved its goal of rescuing the politician and the military began their persecution of the subversive group that had managed to escape through the mountains. In an attempt to avoid another encounter with the army, the guerrillas found a secret shortcut that led to the lower part of the village near Martha's farm. However, they had no idea that the army was waiting for them there, and they fell head-on into their trap. The next confrontation would leave considerable victims on the insurgent side. In an act of desperation, the rebels fled to the nearest house, which happened to be the main house where Martha, Moisés and Jaime were. Within minutes, they had made Martha's house and its surroundings their refuge and point of defense against the army.

Due to this desperate act by the Guerillas, the army's commanding officer quartered off the area around the main house. This was done as a safety precaution so that Christopher and the entire farm staff could not enter the area until the end of the confrontation. The army surrounded the place and tried to take the rebels by surprise, but they were attacked by a shower of bullets, cylinder bombs and MGL grenades. That fateful afternoon the Guerrillas would take Margarita hostage, the young woman responsible for housekeeping and the only employee in Martha's home. The moment the shots rang out, she ducked, running into the kitchen and hid under the sink. Martha and Moisés were worried about her, while they hid with their son in the master bedroom. From there, they could hear the crowd of rebels in the living room and just outside the house firing at the army.

Within minutes, the beautiful and peaceful house had been transfigured into a space impregnated by fear, violence and chaos. A sense of doom began to build within the walls of the house. One of the guerrillas found Margarita and took her hostage while pointing an AK 47 rifle at her. He warned her that if the army didn't back off, they would murder her. When

Moisés heard this, he could see the leader of the group from the window. It was Ulises, the ex-administrator who had been in love with Martha. Moisés's chest tightened with worry and his breathing became shallow. He remembered how Ulises had sworn revenge on Martha years ago for rejecting him. Moisés could hear the insurgent speaking to Margarita. "Joven!" he exclaimed. "Are there more people in the house?" Margarita was overcome by fear. "Sí Señor!" she responded, shaking with fright. "Martha, the owner of the house, her husband Señor Moisés and their son Jaime are in the house." Ulises let the young woman go and immediately ordered several of his men to search all the rooms in the main house, "Bring them to me alive!" he demanded. "But if they resist, kill them!"

At that moment Martha and Moisés understood that their lives were in imminent danger. Their survival instinct took over and they instantly locked the door and blocked it with the furniture in the room. Martha then took a 765 pistol and several extra boxes of bullets out of the cabinet and Moisés armed himself with a Winchester caliber 16 shotgun and an ammo bag that would hold 25 bullets. Jaime, who amazingly continued sleeping despite all the commotion, was moved carefully to the corner of the room furthest from the window and the door. Meanwhile, the guerrillas began to search one room after another. When they arrived at the door of the master bedroom, they found it locked. The guerillas, motioned to the others to knock down the door, as they were certain the couple and son were inside. They tried to kick the door open, but were unsuccessful. One bandit then went up onto the roof and began to lift the sheet metal. Martha immediately stopped him by firing shots at the ceiling. Another insurgent tried to get in through the window but was injured by a shot from Moisés's shotgun.

Hearing the shooting from inside the bedroom, the commanding officer from the army ordered the troops to cease fire since there were civilians inside the house. The army immediately ceased their onslaught on the house. As the minutes passed, the insurgents attack on the couple became more aggressive; the guerrillas were determined to break into the room and reach Moisés and Martha, who were prepared to defend themselves until death. Desperate, because they still hadn't managed to capture Moisés and Martha, the insurgents decided to focus their attack on the window, the most vulnerable point of entry. They attacked in mass. At the time of this onslaught, Jaime woke up and began to cry and Martha ran to him, scooping him up into her arms. At that very moment, the guerrillas ran towards the back of the house. When the army commander officer saw them, he ordered his army to attack the insurgents and they killed several of the guerrillas and wounded others. In the agony of his death, one of the insurgents managed to throw a grenade through the windowpane of the master bedroom. When Moisés saw the grenade, like a feline, he leapt towards Martha and Jaime in order to cover them with his body. But it was too late. Meer seconds before reaching them, the grenade exploded.

As the room went up in flames, the army began a new assault on the house, producing a chaos of blood and fire. As a result, eight guerrillas would die, six were wounded and others were captured. On the army's side, a non-commissioned officer and three soldiers were wounded.

The military scoured the house and found Martha's lifeless body; the grenade had penetrated her skull with shrapnel. Jaime and Moisés were seriously injured, but maintained their vital signs. They were carefully lifted from the debris and driven with haste to the local hospital. Jaime's small body could not withstand the his injuries and he died on the operating table. Due to the nature and severity of Moisés's wounds, he was flown by helicopter to a private clinic in Medellín. The surgeons began operating on him immediately and extracted the splinters of shrapnel that saturated his wounds. After several surgeries, his body managed to recover all of his vital signs.

However, Moisés remained unaware of his wife and son's death. It was only several months after this cruel episode that he would learn about the tragedy through his friend Christopher.

His Body in a Vegetable State

After his final surgery, Moisés entered a comatose state that lasted ninety five days. While in this state, his friends gave Martha and their son a Christian burial and held the funeral. Every mourner waved a white handkerchief as a protest against the violence that had robbed them of their lives. Reporters arrived at the scene shortly after the violent conflict ended. The news was transmitted by satellite all over the world, exposing a senseless war's tragedy and horrors.

Meanwhile, Moisés continued living his own tragedy. Internally, he struggled against death. The hope and yearning to be with his wife and son and have them in his arms gave him the strength to find his way out of a dark labyrinth. During his coma, many people visited him, including those who lived abroad. El señor Federico and his wife volunteered to provide anything that Moisés needed, including money, blood and if necessary, to be transferred to a hospital or clinic in another nation. The day Federico visited, he arrived escorted by a dozen bodyguards. He was very worried about Moisés's state, and visited the hospital for eight days straight, hoping Moisés would show some sign of recovery. The night before his departure, Federico talked to Christopher. "I have to go tomorrow", he said, "but if Moisés needs help of any kind, please don't hesitate to call me. It doesn't matter what he needs or the cost. I'll never forget the day Moisés saved my family. He's the reason I'm alive". Mayra, his first love, would also visit Moisés. After nine years without seeing him, she had heard about the tragedy that had befallen him and his family. His closest friends, Rocio, Joel, Charles, Angela and la Señora Bridget were also present and together they prayed for his recovery.

But it was Christopher and Gustavo who were fully aware of Moisés's dire circumstances. They were responsible for taking care of the funeral costs, the bills from the clinic and continued to take care of the factory and farm. They had contracted workers to repair Martha's house that had been nothing but a heap of rubble after the attack.

Hours later, when Moisés emerged from his coma, he would learn of his most recent tragedy. His body was beginning to respond to the medication and his left hand began to move very slowly. He woke up, a few minutes later, to the familiar sound of a heartbeat, but even more high-pitched. Gradually he opened the eyes and startled, he began to look around. He felt disoriented and wondered why he was in a hospital bed. "What the hell am I doing here?" he asked in the loudest voice he could muster. Christopher heard Moisés's voice for the first time in months.

"Moisés!" he exclaimed, his voice filled with joy and relief.

"You're awake; that's so good! You can't imagine how relieved I am that you've finally come out of the coma. I had begun to lose hope." A series of questions tumbled out of Moisés. "Why am I here? Where are Martha and Jaime? Are they okay?" But before Christopher could answer him, they were interrupted by the doctors, who had entered the room. After checking all of Moisés's vital signs, they ordered the nurse to give Moisés medicine in order to calm his anxiety and help him rest. Then, the director of the clinic called Christopher outside of the room and suggested that he refrain from telling Moisés what had happened to his family until the drug had taken effect.

Next morning when Christopher came back to visit, he found Moisés talking to a psychologist. She seemed to be preparing Moisés for the terrible news. When Christopher saw his friend, he noticed that he was far more relaxed than the previous night. "I feel like you're hiding something from me", he said. "Please tell me what's going on, Christopher". "I'm so sorry Moisés, but I don't know how to begin." Christopher said, concern emanating from his eyes.

"Start where you want!" said Moisés, with optimism. "I need to know where my family is and what has happened since I've been in a coma. Why aren't they here?" Before Christopher began to tell him what happened, he asked Moisés let him speak without interruption until he had finished. Seconds later, with an expression of despair etched in his face, he began to divulge the terrible news to Moisés.

"Your odyssey began the afternoon you were defending your family." Chirstopher said. He paused; wave of melancholy swept over him. "Martha and you faced the guerrillas who had tried to take you hostage. During the confrontation, you were wounded from the shrapnel of a grenade. You were brought to this clinic where you underwent several surgeries to remove these fragments from your body. The surgeons were able to remove several of the pieces of shrapnel, but one of them has remained incrusted between two tendons and will need to be operated on in the next while. The doctors saw how complicated this surgery would be and decided to wait. They have also been worried by a fragment that was embedded near the spinal column and were forced to abort this operation twice because it was extremely dangerous, since the metal could produce paralysis. I decided to sign a document for them to perform the surgery despite the risks involved. After that operation, you entered into a coma for ninety five days. During that time you were never alone. Many friends came to be with you and offer you their support, including me. I've been here the whole time.

"Why aren't Martha and Jaime here?", Moisés demanded, certain now that something bad had happened. "I need to see them, talk to them, hug and kiss them." He said, unable to wait anylonger.

"This is so difficult for me to convey", stammered Christopher with despair, knowing the grief he would cause Moisés. "You can't imagine how much it pain's my soul to tell you. But as your friend, I can't keep the truth from you any longer." Chrishopher took a deep breath. "Martha and Jaime were killed by the same grenade that injured you that fateful afternoon."

"No, no, it can't be!" Moisés cried out. "Why them God... Why?" He pleaded looking up. "Why not take my life and allow them to live? You know that it was only my hope of being with them that enabled me to resist death. Now I'm dead. I have no reason to live anymore."

With tears streaming down his face, Moisés got up, pulled out the IV and then with some difficulty, began staggering out of the clinic. Physically he was very weak from his wounds, but now the pain in his soul had left him without air in his lungs. For that reason, the nurses and doctors didn't attempt to prevent his efforts. They knew that he couldn't withstand more than a few minutes on his feet. However, Moisés found strength in the deepest part of his being and continued to walk unsteadily towards the door of the clinic. Christopher and a couple of the nurses followed him.

"Moisés, please listen to me!" Christopher yelled after him. "You're not able to walk yet. Your wounds need to heal. You need to stay here to get physical therapy and recover". But Moisés was screaming uncontrollably at this point, unable to listen to reason. "Please! Leave me alone, and to hell with healing and therapy. I don't want to live anymore!", he shouted.

Minutes later, Moisés had not only managed to get down the long hallway of the clinic and reach the door but had exited onto the busy street outside. His idea was to launch himself in front of a passing truck, but at that very instant, Christopher grabbed him by the shoulders and pulled him back. "Moisés please, you can't do anything to change the past" he said. "If you commit suicide, your family won't be revived. Wherever they are, they know that you fought for their lives until the last moment. You put your life at risk for them in order to protect them, but circumstance prevented you, and there was nothing you could have done. You shouldn't feel any guilt for what happened. It's true that fate has taken them from you, but you should always remember them as if they were still alive. Even if you no longer wish to live, you should know where the remains of your loved ones are. Let me help you and I'll take you to where they rest in peace."

Moisés listened to Christopher and he felt his words calm him. His impulsive desire to commit suicide dissipated. But at that very instance, a new feeling took hold of him; that of revenge. He would form a self-defence group in order to hunt down the commander guilty of the attack on his family, he thought to himself. Finding Ulises and seeking revenge would be his only incentive to continue living. But even with these thoughts, Moisés was still exhausted and lacked strength. At that moment his body collapsed to the ground. Immediately, the nurses came to help him, and tried to convince him to stay for a time at the clinic in order to heal and recover his strength. But he was insistent on visiting his family's grave site and they left the decision up to Christopher.

Minutes later, Christopher decided to take Moisés to the cemetery. Moisés leant on his friend for support as they walked very slowly to the parking lot. There, Christopher took a credit card out of his wallet and put it in Moisés's pocket. They went to find a place to eat and buy cloths since Moisés was still in his pajamas. Before they left the city, Moisés returned to the clinic to be checked by the doctor who agreed that Moisés would be okay to travel. However, he emphasized the importance of returning to the clinic after the trip to undergo rehabilitation and for the pending surgery in order to remove the remaining fragment of shrapnel lodged between his tendons.

A few hours later, as they were boarding an airplane to San Carlos, Moisés's countenance had changed. He was in a more positive mood. Once the plane landed in San Carlos they took a taxi to the cemetery "La esperanza".

Upon their arrival at the cemetery's entrance, Moisés bought a few bouquets of roses, and Christopher accompanied him to the place where his most loved beings, so vital to his life, had been buried. Moisés found two beautiful tombs there. His wife's grave stone had an aluminum plate with a beautiful dedication engraved in her memory, which included Moises's name as her loving husband. His son's grave stone, right beside Martha's, included a bronze statue of his son riding his pony. Both tombs were beautifully maintained and surrounded by fresh flowers. Christopher admitted to Moisés that he wasn't responsible for the floral arrangements. Whenever he came to visit the graves, he found fresh flowers.

Beside the tombs, Moisés wept and asked questions that only God could answer. Ironically, he found out from Christopher that Ulises's tomb was also in that same cemetery. The bastard directly responsible for the death of his family had been killed by the army. With that knowledge Moisés's plan for revenge dissolved.

Christopher waited patiently for Moisés a few meters away, until Moisés was ready to leave. When Moisés got up and began to walk away, Christopher attempted to accompany him. "Please, Christopher, I need to be alone." Moisés said in a voice laboured due to his sobbing. "I need to think about what I'm going to do with my life." Christopher humbly moved to the side, but not before reminding him that he would have to return to the hospital to begin rehabilitation.

That night, Moisés locked himself in his hotel room, and alone, flooded by memories of the past, he consumed two bottles of whisky; this would mark the beginning of fifteen months of acute alcoholism. After his first drunken stupor, came others and others, and soon he needed generous doses of alcohol to get through the day. Weighed down by self-pity, he rambled aimlessly through the streets like a vagabond. In those days, only liquor could numb his pain enough to go on living. Moisés drank to forget the fateful events that had stripped his life of meaning. However, the sharp pain in his right leg would be a constant reminder of his most recent tragedy.

Christopher was aware of the destructive path Moisés had taken and refused to give up on his friend. Several times a week he visited Moisés in his hotel room and tried to convince him to go to a rehabilitation center. But Moisés always resisted, mostly because he spent the majority of his time inebriated with a handful of friends from the area who shared the same vice. To his new friends, Moisés was like a guardian angel sent from heaven. His experience as a bodyguard gave him the ability to defend them and he also paid for their alcohol with the credit card Christopher had given him. When his friends were hungry, Moisés would also buy them food, although this rarely happened since tequila had become their principal source of protein. Those who knew them well would say that it wasn't blood that ran through their veins but alcohol.

Christopher became increasingly worried about Moisés and the condition he was living in. He would check on Moisés to make sure he maintained some level of hygiene, put on a fresh change of clothes, shaved and had an occasional bath. He didn't want Moisés to be mistaken for a homeless man and risk being executed by a group called "La mano negra" or

"The black hand". This was an illegal group hired by wealthy people to "clean" the city of the unwanted. They scoured the streets killing homeless people, petty thieves and drug addicts. As a precaution, Christopher insisted that Moisés get his life together, but he paid him no attention.

Days after Christopher had tried to convince Moisés yet again, a new fatal episode would transpire. Two of Moisés's alcoholic friends were found dead in a garbage bin, both tortured and killed with a bullet to the head, an action known locally as a "coup de grace". The macabre discovery sobered Moisés. He instantly decided to leave and distance himself from danger. That same afternoon, Moisés traveled to the neighbouring city of Medellín, where he remained several days without one alcoholic beverage, but his desire to drink and the searing pain in his leg, would prove stronger than his will power. Incapable of tolerating the debilitating pain, he once again relapsed into alcoholism. However, this time the path would spiral down until he hit rock bottom.

Meanwhile, his friend Christopher had become frantic due to his friend's sudden disappearance and searched for him in every corner and back alley of San Carlos. While Christopher desperately tried to find him, Moisés's existence had deteriorated to a point that he was considered a "pariah", "un desechable" or society's waste. His disheveled appearance produced pity in some and reminded others of the destructive effects of alcoholism. Moisés would exist in this precarious state for a few more weeks.

In the meantime, Rocio had heard the news from Christopher. Upon hearing of Moisés's disappearance she immediately packed her bags and traveled to San Carlos to join him in the search for their friend.

Nobody knew for sure if it was by chance or fate that led to the eventual amending of Moisés's soul after he had been cruelly robbed over and over of those he loved most.

Fate it seemed, wanted to give him a new opportunity. This opportunity would be decisive in the Moisés's life, as he would be rescued from despair's abyss and he would learn to be a positive force in the world and rescue many from a cursed existence.

At this point in his story, Moisés paused, a wave of nostalgia overtaking him, clouding his eyes. Then he continued, recounting how his friends had searched for him everywhere, in every neighbouring town of San Carlos, without luck. Eventually they ended up in the capital of Medellín, in whose streets Moisés lay unconscious.

Saturated with alcohol and suffering from the intense pain in his right leg, Moisés had lost consciousness many hours ago. Fortunately he was located very close to the central Bus Station, the exact place where Rocio and Christopher would begin their search that morning. As Rocio and Christopher searched the back alleys by the Bus Station on foot, they happened to pass two drunk people and heard one cry out to the other: "Moisés is dying, and we can't do anything about it!" Hearing those words sparked hope in them. They ran to the end of the ally and there they found Moisés curled up in a fetal position among empty whiskey bottles. He was unconscious, without vital signs and on the verge of death.

Christopher and Rocio immediately waved down a taxi and the driver pulled up beside them. Together they lifted Moisés's lifeless body into the back seat of the vehicle and ordered the driver to take them with haste to the nearest private hospital. At the hospital they initially didn't want to treat Moisés due to his appearance and because he lacked identification and insurance. But when Christopher clarified that he was Moisés's friend and would take him under his own insurance, they agreed to treat him.

Apparently the temporary loss of Moisés's vital signs was a defense mechanism produced by his body. After the surgeons removed the shrapnel that had been lodged for many months between the tendons in his leg, the specialist told them that Moisés was very fortunate and had ironically only survived the infection due to the high percentage of alcohol circulating in his blood.This had prevented the spread of the infection, avoided gangrene and the need to amputate his leg.

Late that afternoon and hours after the surgery, Moisés woke up. He felt different. Although his leg was sore and he was groggy from the anesthesia, it was as if a huge weight had been lifted from his body. When he looked in the mirror, he also saw that his beard had been shaven and he was wearing a clean pair of pyjamas. He realized that he was no longer the same person he had been the previous months. He was deeply impacted by the loyalty of his friends and their determination to save him from self-destruction. He felt the value of friendship, one that hadn't abandon him even in the most difficult times in his life.

Moises's recovery would be full of surprises. Earlier that afternoon Rocio had run into Mayra, Moisés's first love, in the clinic's cafeteria. The old friends hadn't seen each other in a long time and were eager to catch up on each other's lives. Rocio recounted the main events of her life to Mayra; José's tragic death, how she had suffered a nervous breakdown and had spent time in a mental institution. Once she had recovered, she explained to Mayra how she met Joel while working at Mariela's Miscellany, the store Moisés's mother had founded. They had eventually fallen in love, she explained, and after a short courtship, she and Joel had married. Now they had a beautiful child, Diseur, she told Mayra. Months after her marriage, she lamented, la Sra. Mariela died but they continued to manage the store that had passed into Moisés's hands. After updating Mayra on her life, Mayra began to relate her own life experiences, but a few seconds later, the happiness in her eyes unexpectedly vanished. "My life has not been as happy as yours" she said with melancholy. "When my parents forced me to separate from Moisés, the man that I loved so deeply, they insisted that I marry a guy that I could never love. He was the president of the University and had good social standing, which was very important to them. They were convinced that I would grow to love him in time. However, right before I finished my specialization in Oncology we divorced. Currently, I am the Director of this clinic. I also founded a non-profit organization that provides psychological treatment and therapy for groups and workshops to individuals that come from families with domestic violence, alcoholism and drug addiction. My clinic also helps street children whom we provide shelter, food, art therapy and other educational programs, which help them survive once they re-enter society. After she finished talking, Mayra paused realizing she hadn't even asked Rocio what had brought her to the clinic. "So what brings you here" Mayra asked. "I'm not here for me, but for my friend Moisés" Rocio answered. Mayra was shocked by the news. "Where is he?" she demanded. "He has been in here since yesterday afternoon" Rocio explained. "He was brought into emergency because of an infection in his right leg and acute alcoholism. We found him unconscious and without vital signs". Mayra was upset but also excited by the news. "I want to see him!" she exclaimed. "I have so much to explain to him! I've been longing to tell him the truth for so long but the last time I saw him, I couldn't tell him what was weighing on my heart because he was in a coma and his life was hanging by a thread".

Without thinking twice, Rocio took her friend by the arm and began to lead her to his room, but suddenly Mayra stopped in her tracks. Her eyes were filled with fear; she was frightened that Moisés wouldn't believe her. Rocio saw the panic in her eyes. "Come on Mayra!" she said optimistically. "Relax and don't worry. I'll come with you." The two went up the elevator and once they reached the third floor, they walked to Moisés's room. Rocio entered the hospital room first. "Moisés!" she said with excitement in her voice. "You won't believe who is here to see you!" Mayra walked into the room cautiously. When Moisés saw her, he cried out with surprise, although he simultaneously felt a sharp pang of pain from the deep wound she had left in his heart. He attempted to supress the resentment that had built up over the years. After an awkward silence, Mayra went up to his bed, hugged him and kissed his cheek. Moisés responded politely and tried not to show his emotions. He had become convinced over the years that Mayra had cut him out of her life in order to hurt him. As Moisés listened to Mayra, he could no longer contain his resentment toward her. He accused her of abandoning him and betraying their love. He also told her directly that since the time she left him, he had suffered a series of fatalities in his life. His life had been besieged by misfortune, beginning with their separation. Even with all the tragedy he experienced, he had always maintained hope that one day she would come back to him and they would be together again. Moisés turned his head away from her, overcome by emotion.

With tears streaming down her cheeks, Mayra placed her hand on his and began divulge all that had weighed on her heart for so long. "I also waited for you," she said softly. "I sent you letters to Rocio's address, but most of them were sent back to me because Rocio wasn't at home due to her health issues. I felt desperate because I hadn't heard any news from you, so I sent a letter with a friend to be delivered to your mother's house, to Mariela's address; however, he betrayed me and gave the letter to my father who persuaded him to lie to me. With his lies he tried to make me believe that you were with another woman and had forgotten all about me. I found it very hard to believe him, so from school, and breaking all the nuns' rules, I called Rocio several times trying to find out the truth from her; but nobody answered my phone calls. Eventually I found out that you had joined the army. Around the same time I found out that everything my "friend" had told me were lies. It was all part of a cruel plot schemed by my father to prevent our union. Once I had finally found out the truth, I had already gotten married" said Mayra with resignation. She felt relieved from saying the words that she had held onto for so long.

"Everything she's telling you is true." Rocio quietly insisted at Moisés's bedside. "I found one of the letters she wrote you, the only letter that wasn't sent back and ending up in her father's hands. It's the same letter that my father showed you at our home so long ago. Remember? You took it on your hands when you came back from the military service, but you never opened or read it. You left it on the table. Luckily, my dad kept it, and when you come back to the village, I'll give it to you. Once you read it, I am sure you'll understand everything that she went through back then and how much she suffered". Mayra interrupted Rocio, wanting Moisés to hear her past sufferings in her own words. She continued with a tone of optimism, and spoke to him as if she were a lawyer making a case in defense of her client's innocence. "Once I had found out the truth," she said, pausing to take a sip of water, "and knowing you were in the army, I couldn't find out anything else. It was as if you had disappeared. Years later, when I was watching the news one night, I heard your name linked to the tragic death of your family. So with a longing to help you, I went to visit you at the hospital many times while you were in a coma. The last time that I visited you, my colleagues told me that you had left the clinic. According to them, the morning you left you were desperate to leave, and they were unable to stop you. Since that date, I was unable to find you until today when by chance I ran into Rocio. I am here because I am still your friend and I want to help you any way I can. I know that you have problems with alcohol. I'm the director and founder of a Foundation that's specialized in treating alcoholism and other addictions".

As Moisés listened to Mayra, he felt the sincerity in her voice and knew that she could help him. So, humbly and with his pride deflated, he allowed her to help him. That same evening, Moisés agreed to leave the hospital and be admitted to the centre Mayra had founded to begin treatment for alcoholism. He took the treatment very seriously and followed all their advice to the smallest detail. As Moisés recalled this period in his life, he remembered that Mayra would visit him every day. During one of these visits, she told him about her life during the time they had been first separated. She explained that after her parents had sent her to the school run by nuns in a town far from their village, she went on to finish high school and attend university. From her first day at university, the Vice Chancellor became captivated by her beauty and soon afterwards, fell in love with her. He was obsessed that she become his wife and without her knowing, contacted her parents. Together they decided that he would be an ideal match for their daughter. Although Mayra, still in love with Moisés, paid the Vice Chancellor's overtures little attention, she eventually relented to her parents' wish, and decided to go out on a date with him.

Months later, disappointed because she hadn't heard from Moisés and losing hope of ever finding him, she eventually accepted the Vice Chancelor's marriage proposal. She would not marry him for love, but rather to please her parents. According to them, as a man of high status, he was the best option for her. He was also politically influential, which would enable her to get ahead quickly in her professional life. They were convinced that in time she would come to love him. However, everything that starts badly ends badly, and without true love, the marriage was doomed to fail. Within a few years their union dissolved and ended in divorce. After that bitter experience, she focused on finishing her studies and soon graduated as a doctor with a specialization in Oncology. Eventually and by her own merits, she became the manager of the hospital where Moisés was being treated.

Moisés recalled that moments after Mayra had opened up to him, she had sighed deeply and confessed: "As you heard Moisés, my life hasn't been a bouquet of roses. I hope you understand now that I'm not the only one who has made errors; you also made mistakes.

That afternoon, after a long talk, the two realized that they had been manipulated by destiny. If, after so many years, fate had decided to give them a new opportunity to be together, they would be foolish to resist it. But first Moisés would have to complete his treatment for alcoholism.

After two months in therapy, Moisés began to feel that he had recovered. He didn't believe there was any sense in continuing with treatment because he had managed to dominate his desire for alcohol to the point that even the smell bothered him. He talked to Mayra about leaving treatment and thanked her. Mayra said good bye to him with a kiss on the cheek. "Will I be seeing you again?", she asked him with some sadness. Moisés looked into Mayra's eyes. "That is very possible", he said. After saying goodbye, Moisés took a taxi to a shopping center in the city center and bought everything he needed for his trip to San Carlos, Antioquia. While in Antioquía, he visited his friend Charles and his family. He expressed his gratitude to them for all the blessings they had given him. Then promised that he would begin to live a normal life again and allow himself to be happy again.

From there, he went to the cemetery and visited Martha and Jaime's graves. He prayed for them there, spoke to them, cried and swore that he would never fall back into alcoholism. When Moisés finished praying to his loved ones and got up to leave, he noticed a lady who wore a black dress and veil approach his wife and son's graves. A boy with a facial scar from a severe burn accompanied her. The lady carried several roses and placed them on the Martha's grave while kneeling down. There, she began to sob and spoke in a low voice pleading to Martha for something that he couldn't quite distinguish. Her emotion and modest behaviour made Moisés wait for her. Once she had finished praying, Moisés approached her. "Excuse me Señora," he said, "did you know the deceased woman?" "Yes, of course!" she answered. "We were distant relatives. I used to call her "Santa Marta" when she was still alive. She was an excellent person and so good to me. The day that my son Alvaro suffered major burns in an accident, she went to the hospital and demanded that he be sent to a specialized clinic in the Capital. Because we were having money problems, she paid for everything; the surgery, the drugs and our stay in Medellín. However, after six surgeries, the skin on his face was delicate and still not healed and the surgeons decided to postpone the last surgical intervention until he had gone through puberty. But unfortunately for him, our benefactor died very young. To express gratitude to her for her remarkable kindness and generosity, we come to visit her grave every Monday. We always bring flowers and pray. We ask Martha, now in heaven, to soften the surgeon's heart so that he would perform the final facial surgery for free. Due to our difficult economic circumstances, his surgery is still pending."

Saddened by her story, Moisés interrupted her. "What is your name Señora?" he asked. "My name's Teresa Escobar", she said. After their conversation, the woman and her son left, but Moisés stayed at the graves for a little longer, pondering how he could help Teresa and her son. Afterward, Moisés went to Martha's farm. Once he arrived, his nostalgia for the past overwhelmed him. Memories of his life with Martha and their son flooded every pore of his body and saturated his soul. He could see Martha and Jaime's images so clearly before him, as if they were still alive, living at the farm. He remembered how she would watch her baby tenderly while riding on his pony and how Jaime would ride by her, throwing her kisses. Moisés was so immersed in the past that he didn·t hear Christopher approach him. Christopher's voice, welcoming Moisés to the farm, startled him back to reality.

After greeting each other, the young man showed Moisés how the farm that had been restored and how the buildings had been repaired following the tragedy. Christopher also talked about some of the changes he made on the farm and to the cheese factory. He showed him the systematization of the milk company and a web page where they advertised the cheese and other milk products and where farmers could buy and sell livestock. Business was flourishing with these technological advances, and Moisés found that both properties were in very good hands. He gave the go-ahead to Christopher to continue managing the farm and business. Christopher was not only a veterinarian, and competent at running the farm but also Martha's adoptive son. Therefore it made sense that he inherited fifty per cent of the profits.

Moisés felt satisfied with the newest developments on the farm. However, he needed to do something for Martha, a humane gesture that would continue her legacy of kindness. So he asked Christopher to have a public notary come to the farm and then to pick up la Señora Teresa Escobar and her son Alvaro in San Carlos, Antioquia. Once they had all arrived, Moisés held a public ceremony to give them thirty-five cows, two stallion bulls, ten hectares of land with ample grass and a small house within the perimeter of the property. The donation was granted on the condition that Teresa and her son would only sell number of livestock that exceeded the original number given to them in addition to their milk production.

Moisés recommended that they join the cooperative in order to manage their new farm.

Once the agreement was signed, Moisés spoke with Christopher about making the arrangements for Alvaro's final surgery in a private hospital in Medellín. Then Moisés, wished them well and said goodbye. From there, he headed to his town, Convención, where an unfinished chapter in his life awaited him.

HIDDEN TRUTH

On the eve Moisés returned to his village, he would learn of two hidden truths. Both would bring him optimism and a new sense of hope. However, as he walked towards Rocio's place, his thoughts were preoccupied. Moisés was thinking about that letter; the letter that according to Mayra, would be decisive in his life and change his perspective on what had occurred between them many years earlier. But before knocking on his friends' door, he paused on the steps outside. He felt nervous about finding out the truth after so many years.

The person who first noticed his presence was his godson, Dirseur. "God father!" !God father!" he cried out with excitement, jumping up and down. Rocio and Joel came running to see who it was. They couldn't believe it when they saw Moisés standing there. They hugged him. Moisés instantly noticed that Rocio was too thin, and wore a haggard expression that wasn't usual in her. "How are you?" he asked with concern, when he had the opportunity to speak to her alone. "Are you having problems with Joel?"

She moved back in surprise. "No, it's nothing! Why are you asking?" she said, nonchalantly. "Because you don't look well", Moisés responded. "Don't worry it's just a migraine that will soon pass," said Rocio, attempting to reassure Moisés."I don't believe you!" Moisés exclaimed, astonished that his dear friend of so many years would hide the truth from him. "I can tell from your face that something's going on. Please tell me the truth." At that moment, she could no longer find the words to keep lying. "Okay Moisés, I'll tell you since you're my best friend and you love me like a sister". Rocio paused and took a breath. "I am ill", she said. "Years ago I contracted an infection in my left kidney but it never worried me. Now I'm worried because at my last doctor's visit, I wasn't feeling well and they sent me to see a specialist. After doing some tests he told me that my left kidney is no longer functioning and that the other kidney is also infected. If the left kidney isn't removed immediately and the other is not treated with strong medication, the disease will kill me. The doctor says if I don't do anything, I only have a year to live. The surgeon also suggested removing both kidneys and undergoing a transplant, although there's the risk that that my body would reject the new organ and I could die in the operating room. The surgery is both risky and extremely expensive. It would cost us five million pesos. That's why Joel has no idea that I'm sick. He senses that something is wrong and keeps asking me, but I make up lies because I don't want to worry him. Just this morning, one of my surgeons called to tell me that they found a donor and to come to the hospital as soon as possible. He wants to start preparing my body for the organ transplant. But the problem is this surgery is not only risky but also costly. I don't want Joel to spend all his savings on me. He would have to spend all the money he's saved up for years on a surgery that I may not even survive. He has been dreaming of having his own farm. I don't want to get in the way of his dreams. At the same time, I think about my child, and I don't want him to lose his mother. All these worries leave me feeling confused. Moisés took Rocio by the shoulders and looked her directly in the eyes and told her she needed to tell Joel what was going on immediately. He told her not to worry and assured her that he would take care of the cost of the transplant. He also tried to convince her that she had to take the risk. There are moments in life when you have to risk your life in order to survive, he explained.

Minutes after their conversation, Joel would learn about Roció's secret. When he heard about the specialist's most recent diagnosis, Joel was completely demoralized. He got up from his chair, and left the room in anguish and despair. When Moisés saw that he was crying, he hugged him and tried to offer some comfort. They talked for several minutes on the sofa; the conversation relaxed him a little. "Remember Joel, not all is lost", Moisés said optimistically. "We must be grateful to God that she has a donor and there is a chance that the transplant will work".

That morning, after Rocio had revealed the truth to her husband, Moisés went to the cemetery to visit his mother's grave. He prayed there for her eternal rest and also said a prayer for Rocio's wellbeing. In the afternoon they began their preparations for their trip to the hospital. Before leaving, Rocio gave Moisés Mayra's letter; the letter that her father had kept for many years. Moisés took it into his hands and before opening it, thought about Mayra for a few seconds. Moisés suddenly felt like a teenager who was in love. He was anxious to read the letter that had been waiting for him almost for ten years. When he unfolded the letter, he was surprised to see a two hundred peso bill inside. The bill was like new, and in the middle of bill, he found a drawing of a heart pierced with an arrow, with the words written below: "You are my passion and I will never stop loving you. I'll love you always, Moisés"

He recalled that he had drawn that heart and written this phrase the day before Mayra's departure long ago when she was forced by her parents to attend school in another town. He also remembered the night her father found them together and he became furious, beating her and tearing up her notebooks. During this moment of upheaval, Mayra quickly retrieved the bill from her personal diary and hid it in the pocket of her jeans, seconds before her father began tearing up her books.

After reading the letter, Moisés understood that the only reason their love story ended was because he hadn't received Mayra's letter on time. Mayra had written the address and date where she wanted to meet with him in her letter. In another part of the letter she also wrote that in the name of their love she was willing to give up her family and give him her virginity. So with those words he knew that he was the first man she wanted to be with. While Moisés was pondering her words, Joel and Rocio finished packing for their trip. When they were ready to leave, Rocio kept coming back to hug and kiss Diseur who would be staying with his grandmother. She wasn't sure if she would see him again due to the risks involved with the kidney transplant.

Moisés still didn't know if the Rocio's illness was destiny or chance, but fate seemed in their favor. The doctor who would be performing the operation was the head specialist at the clinic where Mayra was Director. Because the medical intervention was difficult, Rocio would be observed by a medical board in order to coordinate up to the finest details. A single error could prove fatal. Joel and Moisés were asked to sign a document certifying that they were in agreement with the risks associated with the operation. So without even having planned it, Moisés would end up in Mayra's office. After signing the document, Joel intuitively left them alone. Moisés took the letter from his pocket and put it in Mayra's hands. "I owe you an apology", he said meekly. She took his hands in hers. "I think what we need is another opportunity", she said. Although he knew Mayra's words were expressed with love and sincerity, it was still too soon for Moisés. The memories of his late wife Martha still flooded his body, like blood coursing through his veins. Her death still obscured the clarity of his soul. Without a doubt, Mayra had stirred the ashes of the past, but even so, Moisés wasn't ready to begin a relationship with her again. But nevertheless something inside him sought her, sometimes inadvertently. He would walk where she might walk or stumble upon her at the clinic while he visited Rocio, whom the doctors were preparing for surgery. Mosiés would engage in conversation with Mayra and on more than one occasion, they went to the Rehab Center Mayra had founded.

After several days of medical tests, the time had come for Rocio's operation. That morning, Joel and Moisés went to the small chapel within the clinic, where they prayed to God for Rocio's welfare and prompt recovery. It took ten hours to complete the kidney transplant and afterward, she was taken to the intensive care unit. Fifteen minutes after relocating Rocio, the head surgeon emerged from the operating room and confirmed that the operation had been a success. When Joel and Moisés, heard those words uttered, their souls seemed to return to their bodies. The surgeon could see their joy and relief. "You can see her, but only from the window because she needs time to recover and can't speak", the surgeon said with optimism.

That night in the midst of their happiness, Mayra invited Joel and Moisés to dinner, but for obvious reasons, Joel found an excuse not to go. He wanted to stay at the clinic close to Rocio and also wished to give Mayra and Moisés some time alone. Therefore, the reservation was made for two. The dinner was pleasant and not without a small dose of romance as Moisés and Mayra reminisced about the past, and spoke of the possibility of rekindling their romance. Afterward, Moisés accompanied Mayra to her apartment and said goodbye to her with a kiss on the cheek. When Mayra felt Moisés's lips brush her cheek, she found his lips and stole a passionate kiss. In a moment of unbridled passion, he embraced and caressed her, igniting sexual desire, however they both resisted their desire.

Several weeks later Rocio had recovered completely and they decided to take a trip to Martha's farm. Mayra also joined them. She hoped to recover the love she and Moisés used to share and also strengthen her friendship with Rocio and Joel. The evening of their arrival, Alvaro, the boy who had suffered the burn on his face was waiting for them. When Moisés saw that the operation had been a success and his face looked completely healed, the scar barely noticeable, he couldn't believe it. Alvaro approached him and thanked him with hugs and tears. He expressed his deep gratitude to Moisés with a big smile. The boy then told him that he planned to study to become a great surgeon one day and treat the people who were most in need. Seeing the boy's new face, hearing his words of thanks and his hope for the future along with Rocio's recovery, filled Moisés with satisfaction. He knew at that moment that he was destined to help others.

That evening, after speaking to Mayra, Moisés decided to work at the Rehab Center that she had founded. Meanwhile, Rocio and Joel were longing to be with their son Diseur and the day after arriving at the farm, they decided to go home. Mayra and Moisés understood that being with their son was the couple's priority and without hesitation they accompanied them to see them off in San Carlos.

His Work at the Foundation and his Third Marriage

It was not long before Moisés had become an active member of Mayra's Foundation in Medellín; this would mark the beginning of a new chapter in his life. Some of his new tasks consisted of steering the patients away from addiction and helping them recover. He would go out onto the streets of Medellín and find those who several months earlier had been his friends; all of them entrenched in alcoholism and other addictions. This was an arduous task, but after many meetings, and many frustrated attempts to convince them, Moisés achieved his goal. Once they had agreed to enter and stay in the program within the institution, he was able to begin their rehabilitation, complimented with group therapy and long sessions of psychoanalysis. The program at the Center sought to eventually integrate their patients into society again.

After several months in treatment, Moisés's group had made so much progress that they were essentially deemed recovered and ready to start a new life. Before leaving, Mayras's Foundation, they gave speech to new addicts entering the program. That day Moisés's group told the new patients about their experiences and the reasons behind their addictions. Moisés found out that three of the five friends that he had brought to the Center had begun drinking alcohol regularly at the age of thirteen. Another patient had been a successful lawyer who had fallen into alcoholism in the past year after losing three consecutive cases. His disappointment led him seek alcohol as a refuge, but instead it only aggravated the situation. As a result, he lost his home, dignity and family. Now, rehabilitated, he hoped to regain what he had lost. Two his former colleagues had just proposed that all of them set up their own law practice. The other guy was a village doctor; he had it all: respect, money and a wife who loved him. However, he made the mistake of falling in love with a young woman, fifteen years younger than him who was far too clever for him. She had the face of an angel but no trace of compassion or kindness. She manipulated him into getting what she wanted until he didn't have a peso left. Disillusioned by her and his own stupidity, he found consolation in alcohol. He thought alcoholism was an addiction he would never overcome, however, thanks to Moisés, he was released from his vice and his life had transformed for the better. Although he was no longer the same prestigious doctor of his past, he had recently received a job offer by the mayor of the town to be the soccer team's new physician. When Moisés heard all of these stories, he became even more motivated to work for all those who needed his help.

In time Moisés became part of the organizing committee of the Center. He began giving lectures and workshops at universities, schools and in neighborhood community centers. His desire to help people with serious problems and his own experiences with alcoholism gave him the sensibility of a blood hound to find those who needed help and devise an individual program for each patient.

Because Mayra and Moisés shared the same cause at the Foundation, they spent a lot of time together. So after a complicated and long road, his passion for Mayra rekindled and over the time they developed a deep love for each other. Their feelings would be consolidated in a ceremony in front of the altar.

On their wedding day, Mayra hoped that her family would attend. However, she decided not to allow their absence to cloud her happiness. In contrast to Mayra's relatives who refused to come out of pride, all of their most loyal friends and many others were present and shared in the happiness of their union. The night of their wedding, Moisés would see that his godson Dirseur had turned into a handsome teenager. Rocio, who was in her final months of pregnancy, stood beside him and Joel was thrilled to become a father again after trying unsuccessfully for several years. Meanwhile, Charles's and his family were doing very well. Charles had become Taekwondo world champion in his category. Christopher, el señor Gustavo, the members of the Cooperative and Don Federico and his family to whom he was always grateful, were also present.

Days after their nuptials, the Foundation directed by Mayra, was presented an award for demonstrating excellence in Human Rights, and Mayra was granted an award of Merit for her great work as the Director, having maintained the institution's high standards to the point that the Center was being used as a model for humanitarian organizations around the world. Ten years later, their marriage continued to be strong and happy. Two precious children were born to them, and although they were extremely busy with work, the ties that bound their family were rooted firmly in their hearts, just like the old Oak tree's roots were rooted deeply in the soil of the village park of Convención.

Moisés ended his story with this image of happiness within his family. However, I was so busy comparing his life experiences with my own, that I didn't even notice when he had got up and left. When I looked up to ask him another question, I didn't seem him anywhere. In the same way he had appeared in my life, he had also vanished, as if by magic.

Six months after my attempt to commit suicide that had been unsuccessful because of Moisés's intervention, I unexpectedly ran into him again. That day, he was giving a lecture at a school. When my wife and me arrived, he was finishing his presentation. He wanted to end his speech with his favorite fable, one that his deceased uncle Antonio used to tell him. "I will end my presentation with a wonderful story of hope", he told his audience enthusiastically.

Six hundred years ago, in a remote land, there was a country called Discord. During the first years of its creation, nothing disturbed the tranquility in this pacific country. No one owned property and its people took equal shares of land and supplies. They never thought to take more than what they needed and would follow the rules with utmost respect.

Years later, a group of people in this land became ambitious and conflict arose among them disrupting its peace. The balance had been broken and the country of Discord was divided into three kingdoms; each kingdom then introduced its own laws and specific rules. The first of these kingdoms was known as Terror, which was governed by a wicked Queen called Violence. In her kingdom, children, young, adults and old people didn't have any respect for their neighbors. Due to their ambition Terror's people started to leave their territory, and kidnap and physically abuse children and women of the other kingdoms to obtain what they wanted. What's more, those who protested against this brutality were suppressed and controlled by violence. It became a place where gunfire dominated the streets.

The people of the kingdom of Terror accumulated resentment due to rising dissidence in other kingdoms. They would hide camouflaged in unsuspecting places, trying to put seeds of evil in the most noble of souls. They were looking for any pretext to create chaos. But what was most disturbing was that many people outside of their territory started to follow their bad example. It became like a plague that spread like wild fire through the land.

The kingdom of Hope was located in the middle of the three kingdoms. It was the biggest of all empires, headed by a noble and optimistic queen, named Hope, the same name as her land. She imagined that she had a powerful army that imposed security and convinced everyone that she would be the winner in the end. However, all of this was Queen Hope's imagination. Her grand army that protected her kingdom was a fantasy she had conjured in her palace.

The third kingdom was called Peace and it was managed by a humble and resourceful queen named Harmony. The fact that her kingdom, and that of Hope lacked an army allowed Queen Violence to penetrate the Kingdom of Hope and attack her kingdom in an attempt control her land. Even so, peace's people never responded to the Violence's aggression. They took refuge in their castle and waited patiently for the invader to leave. They knew that despite a fierce attack, the evil queen could not vanquish their kingdom.

Queen Hope, sad, incapable and lonely, could not intervene in favor of her pacific neighbour. From her balcony she was limited to observing the atrocities left in Queen Violence's wake. Terror, she lamented, would spread through the world. Following the cruel attack, Queen Harmony sent several of her emissaries to the kingdom of Terror in an attempt to try and persuade Queen Violence to change her attitude, but in an act of retaliation to their noble request, the evil queen beheaded the messengers and sent their heads back to the Kingdom of Peace. Violence continued her attacks without cessation, day after day and year after year.

Queen Harmony decided she needed some support against her cruel neighbour and searched for an ally. She approached Queen Hope and asked her to join forces with her to help achieve her objective. After Queen Hope agreed, all of the citizens of the Kingdom of Peace's were filled with love and courage. Although this alliance made the land of Peace stronger, the violent attacks prevailed.

Years later, after many efforts to end the rampant violence, without result, Queen Hope became disappointed. She had hoped to see an end to the reign of Terror, but it continued. Sad and tired, she went to bed. During the night, she dreamt vividly and saw her land suspended in time. Amazed, the Queen walked out onto the balcony and looked out over her kingdom. She could see Harmony and Violence walking together hand in hand toward her castle. Excited, Queen Hope ran down to meet them, opening the door of her fortress optimistically and filled with a renewed hope for peace. The three queens walked into the main hallway, sat down around of the table and there, like sisters, began to talk. Queen Harmony looked at Queen Violence in the eyes. "Violence", she asked. "Why is your soul filled with revenge?" "My soul was as noble and pure as yours", answered Queen Violence. "However, one day, dark forces invaded my heart and turned off the light of love, planting evils seeds in my soul that germinated the fruit of resentment in me. That hatred and pain began to course like blood through my veins making me believe that the world was not good enough for me. Because of my astute arrogance, I looked down upon humble people and sought their downfall through violence". The leaders of the Kingdoms of Peace and Hope were dismayed to hear her words. "We don't like your way of thinking because our souls are opposite to yours", Queen Harmony said. "Our virtue is to be kind and full of compassion. These qualities are necessary to transform this world into a better place. But it's not too late for you, Queen Violence. Despite your resentment and hurt, it's possible to change with us as your examples, and we can help you calm your sorrows and be free of your resentment. Together we can look for a solution to your diabolical nature. We are sure that if you purge the evil from your mind and body, the void in your heart can open up to be filled with love and you will be humbled", Queen Harmony insisted.

After their intense discussion, Queen Violence slowly came to the conclusion that Queen Harmony and Queen Hope's words were not unwise. She was tired and ragged from terror and also desired to live in a world of joy and peace. So queen Violence stripped her body of evil and her stone heart instantly began to soften. Soon her subjects followed her example, and they also dismissed all evil from their souls forever. They subsequently welcomed humility and love into their lives.

Queen Hope then observed the territory of Discord return to peace. Evil vanished from the land as if by a magic spell. She looked with contentment as the exiles returned to their lands and watched how guns became silent and bullets became obsolete. Nations were no longer at war and women and children were no longer abused. In her dream she observed that in the territories of Discord, protests and starvation were problems of the past. It was as if the kidnappings, greed and ambition had never existed.

Queen Hope awoke from her dream with joy rising in her heart. She rushed to her balcony and hoped to see her dream materialize in reality. However, deeply disappointed, she realized that the violent conflict not only continued but was getting worse. Her dream had been nothing but a fantasy. She was so upset that she crawled back into bed pulling the covers over her head. She preferred to return to her dream and hold on to the illusion of peace and harmony. Perhaps, she thought, the next time she awoke, peace would rein over the land and supress the actions of evil Queen Violence.

Although Queen Hope's dream will never materialize in reality, this does not mean that she and Queen Harmony should be resigned to retreat into a world of fantasy and hide from the horrors of reality. Rather, they must continue to struggle to spread seeds of love and peace and find solutions within the misery and terror...

With those words, Moisés's voice trailed off and he finished his speech. The audience rose from their chairs and gave him a resounding applause to show their gratitude and respect. Many wished to shake his hand or take a photo with him. I took my wife by the waist and we began to make our way through the crowd of students toward Moisés. Minutes later, when we had reached the podium, my wife expressed her surprise. Moisés was quite small in stature for all he had accomplished. "Are you Moisés?", she asked. "Sí, linda!" he responded. "How can I help you?" "You have incredible charisma and the power of persuasion", she told him. "You managed to transform my husband's life for the better and although I longed to make these same changes in him, I always failed. Due to the radical change you inspired, I can say that Hansel isn't the same person he was. I'm not the only one who has seen the profound change in him; all of his friends and family have noticed it too." She then thanked him. Her words filled Moisés with a sense of satisfaction. "I left a legacy of struggles and joys in Hansel" Moisés said. "To have contributed to the improvement of his personal life gives me great satisfaction. But my journey does not end here; I will continue with my role as mediator so that others, like Hansel, have a second chance at life" he continued. "You'll see, now he'll also provide support for those that were in a similar situation to his. I'm convinced that if we create a chain of support, once we have departed this world, we'll have left it a little better then we found it".

In the midst of our conversation, Moisés was interrupted by security officers from the school. They warned the people present not leave the building as there was a shootout taking place between the police and criminals who were attempting to rob one of the jewelry stores in the area. According to the security guard, the robbers' plan was undermined by the security guards at the jewelry store who had notified police. When the criminals tried to escape, the police had already caught up to them. Without knowing where to turn, they burst into a kindergarten and took the children and teachers hostage. Right now the robbers were threatening to kill the teachers if the military police did not retreat immediately.

Minutes after the warning, the police allow all the people inside the school to leave the building with caution and returned home. Then they closed off the area in order to negotiate with the criminals and demand they free the hostages unharmed. In exchange, they would provide some money and a helicopter for them. The authorities thought the bandits would agree to this, but soon things began to get out of hand as their demands proved much higher. Forty-eight hours after the outlaw's had taken the school children hostage, they had almost run out of food in the kindergarten. The robbers became stressed by the children's crying and accepted that provisions be brought in by the Red Cross. The criminals demanded that the food be left outside the main door, behind the Venetian blinds. They also insisted that when the food arrived, all civilians should be no less than eighty meters from them because they didn't wish to kill anyone due to their curiosity.

But time was running out and the two sides still hadn't come to an agreement. The criminals were trying to take advantage of circumstances and demanded five hundred million pesos or they would kill one of the children. They gave a period of seventy-two hours for the government to deliver the stipulated amount. The bandits threatened that if their agreement wasn't met in this time period, they would kill one of their captives.

The next day passed far too quickly for relatives and friends of the hostages. There were only eight hours remaining to the ultimatum and then the criminals would begin to kill one of their victims if their demands weren't met. A few hours before the fateful time, there seemed to be commotion inside. Minutes later, four of the five criminals approached the main entrance where one of the kindergarten teachers stood, holding a piece paper in her hands in front of the Venetian blinds. The police could see the bandit's guns pointed at her from behind as she was told to read the criminals' new demands. They first reminded police that the deadline was quickly approaching. Therefore, as a security measure for themselves, they demanded five parachutes and a helicopter with a civilian pilot. Then, wanting to secure their escape, they reiterated their threat, demanding a response to their request by the stipulated deadline or the first victim, a teacher, would be killed. If their request was still not met after killing one captive they would wait one hour and if they still had not received the money from the government, they would continue killing their captives, beginning with one of the children. When the relatives of the prisoners heard the radical actions the criminals were prepared to take, they were filled with anguish and despair. Overcome by fear, some began to panic.

The authorities immediately stationed snipers in the surrounding buildings and ordered them to take action. But they reported to their commander that it was impossible to act because they observed through the only window without Venetian blinds that each one of the bandits had a child tied on their back and another on their chest in order to create a human shield. As each minute passed, the agony and suffering of the hostages increased, just as it did for the relatives knowing that the hostages in the kindergarten were only a few hours from the deadline and the authorities had still not confirmed they would meet their request. When only an hour remained of the seventy-two hours, the aircraft and the money had still not arrived at the agreed site. According to the criminals, if police did not meet all aspects of the agreement, one hostage would die. Although the bandits' threats were real, the police were not worried, believing they had the situation under control.

While the deadline was quickly approaching and the tension was mounting between the bandits and police. During the 72 hour ultimatum, Moisés visited me a couple of times. During his final visit he asked me if I'd like to be an active member of the Rehabilitation Center where he worked with Mayra, an offer that I accepted immediately. So at that moment I became his friend and partner in his cause. From then on, I would accompany him to his presentations. He told me that due to personal commitments, he would only stay in the city for one more week and would therefore most likely find out what happened with the kidnapping of the children by the news, radio, television and street reviews.

Up until now, Moisés had observed the many attempts made by the authorities to reach an agreement with the assailants. However, the criminals stood firmly by their demands and refused to negotiate; for them it was all or nothing. Due to the offenders' ultimatum, the people who approached the main entrance of the kindergarten with the intention to communicate with the criminals would be shut out whether they were police officers or not. Suddenly the final minute had ticked by and the church clock struck the eleven hour that marked the fatal deadline and would reveal the outcome of this odyssey.

Seconds later, several gunshots could be heard; apparently one teacher had been killed. The fear between the relatives and friends, who were a few meters from the kindergarten, rose to hysteria. Many of them desperately attempted to launch themselves across the barricade, but security forces forced them back. In the midst of the commotion, relatives, police and onlookers like me, could see a man emerge from the crowd. He was in his underwear, in order to show that he was an unarmed civilian. He was also carrying a sign that read: "I have lived enough, but they are only children and are entitled to live their lives. So, take me as your hostage instead of one of them and if there should be another victim, let me be next." That man was Moisés; he had somehow managed to evade the security rope and barricade placed by the authorities. Now without obstacles in his way, he had slowly made his way up to the main entrance. In a matter of minutes, he was in reach of the bandits' bullets, who now were pointing their guns at him from inside of the children's school.

Bystanders, police, radio and television journalists, who remained in the area, waited helplessly for the criminals to shoot him. Aware of this newest development, the cameramen observed that the events, nevertheless, didn't unfold as expected. The daring man who had reached the entrance, grabbed onto the latch that opened the door. Once inside, he disappeared behind the Venetian Blinds, closing the door behind him. Seconds later, one of the criminals carrying a child on his back and another on his chest, approached him. He aimed a gun at Moisés's head and ordered him to be handcuffed. After ensuring that Moisés couldn't cause problems for them, the criminals pushed him into the main hall as one of the evildoers pressed the barrel of a gun into his back. Moisés could almost see all of the hostages from there, except the teacher who had read the statement hours earlier.

From the moment he had entered the school, Moisés could see a total of five bandits in the main room, all masked with balaclavas. He also counted a total of sixteen children and three teachers. The teachers were doing their best to distract many of the children, while the rest of them had been tied onto the bandits, becoming their human shields. Each of the criminals had been assigned a post; two guarded the adults and infants that were playing in the living room while a third bandit interrogated Moisés, still handcuffed and sparsely clothed. The other two bandits watched for any suspicious movement in the back garden. They used convex mirrors to see everything that was happening around the school's perimeter.

Moisés observed several bullet holes in one of the bathroom doors. But since he didn't see any blood, he assumed that the shots were meant as a fear tactic. The criminals wanted to demonstrate to the authorities that they were negotiating with professional killers and not amateurs, he rationalized. The bandits thought that this would help convince the police to give in to their demands. Moisés suspected that they most likely had a woman locked in the bathroom pretending to be dead. They were setting the stage for the snipers, whom they suspected had found a way to observe them. They also were aware that without a body as evidence, the authorities would doubt that someone had died. Moisés was convinced at that moment that the gun shots had been a set up and he began to search for clues by talking to the criminal guarding him. Like a psychologist, Moisés got him to reveal his past little by little. In a few minutes, he began to concede details about his life as a criminal. He admitted to Moisés that in all his years as a thief, this experience was the most frustrating because all their previous assaults had been successful, so there had been no need to make use of arms in order to achieve their goal. All their previous robberies had been planned months in advance and carried out very accurately. Due to the way they maneuvered themselves, explained the bandit, the authorities seem to think they were dangerous criminals. But in reality they were not murderers, nor extremists. On the contrary, he insisted, each of them possessed a big heart. Part of their profits obtained from the thefts was always given to people in need. In poor neighborhoods, the neediest would receive medicine, money for doctor's visits, and coverage for expensive surgeries. Sometimes they even paid for funeral costs of those deceased. He went on to say that they always robbed those who had too much money in order to distribute the wealth to the less fortunate. Although they recognized their actions were illegal and wrong, it was a way for them to escape their own despair and inability to deal with their own failures. He recognized the irony of how this most recent robbery could be the sequel of a film that they had watched. They hoped, that just like in many films they had seen, the criminals would come away with what they demanded. They believed that by taking children hostage and kindergarten teachers, they would find an easy way out and everyone would escape unharmed. They thought the authorities would take their threats more seriously and succumb to their demands, since children's lives were on the line. However, as their time passed and the hour of their ultimatum came without any of their demands met, they realized that these ideas were based on fantasy and in reality, events would unfold very differently.

After listening to the guard attentively, Moisés could not only sense this man's emotional instability, but that of the entire group. He decided to try and help them. What the guard had revealed to him made Moisés think that the robbers were incapable of killing anyone. They were much less dangerous than they portrayed themselves to be. With a sense of optimism, Moisés asked them if he could act as mediator between them and the authorities and look for a solution to the conflict. Moisés didn't want them to believe that he thought their actions were justified, rather he hoped that the hostages, criminals and he would emerge from the situation alive. He also felt that he could not condemn them without giving them the opportunity to reconsider their own errors. After analyzing the situation, Moisés promised them that he would help them with the court case and eventual trial if they were detained by police, but only if they swore under oath, not to harm the children.

When the offenders first listened to Moisés, they thought it was a joke, but minutes later they found reason in what he was saying. They understood now that he was providing them with a way to escape their predicament unharmed, and so realizing that they would never obtain their demands from the authorities, they relented and accepted Moisés's proposal. Immediately after their agreement, they took off Moisés's handcuffs and gave to him shorts and T-shirt. Then, they announced that he be their spokesman, and gave him the white flag to go ahead and attempt to negotiate an agreement with the authorities. They agreed to release the hostages in order to get a future sentence reduction.

While these events were unfolding in the kindergarten, the relatives of the prisoners remained ignorant of the agreement reached with Moisés inside the building. They had begun to lose hope of seeing their loved ones again. They were resigned to the fact that the killing spree would continue since time had run out for the hostages and no requests had been met. The relatives' watches ticked relentlessly as time marched cruelly toward the fateful hour when the next person would fall victim. But when the clock reached the next hour, surprisingly no gun shots rang out. The relatives looked at their watches anxiously as the minutes and then hours passed without further incident within the kindergarten. Now five hours had passed since the stipulated limit to the criminals' ultimatum.

Suddenly the front door flew open and through the metal lattice, everyone could see the daring man who hours earlier, had made his way into the building. But now he wore cloths and he carried a child in his arms. The site of Moisés produced a sudden release of tension among the family members. They could see that this was a gesture of good will from the criminals and reflected a change in their strategy. The relatives of the hostages were now filled with new hope. When Moisés reached the police security fence, journalists

Héctor Sanguino

surrounded him and tried to take his picture, which would headline the front pages of all national and local newspapers. However, the authorities pushed them back and immediately took the infant under their protection. With haste, they sent the boy in an ambulance to the nearest medical clinic to check his state of health. Once it had been determined that the child was in perfect condition, he was handed over to his parents. Immediately afterward, Moisés, criminals' emissary, began to negotiate with the authorities in order to come to an agreement to the new conditions and ensure the release of all of the captives. The thieves wished to negotiate directly with the judge and prosecution team and have their agreement in writing that confirmed a sentence reduction for not harming any of the captives. In exchange for giving themselves up to the authorities, they demanded that their sentence be reduced in accordance to hours of work or study in prison and that they would be prosecuted only under murder charges and the possession of illegal weapons.

This ultimatum was planned by the outlaws in advance, designed to be put it into action in case their original ultimatum didn't work. In the end, the alternate plan would work out for the criminals, especially since Moisés didn't let the authorities know that the teacher, whom everyone thought dead, was in fact still alive inside the bathroom. After listening to the bandits' proposal through the voice of Moisés, the Police commissioner demanded that they release all of the infants along with the body of the killed teacher as a condition to their agreement. The bandits, who were listening to the negotiations on their mobile phone, responded immediately. As proof that the children were unharmed they agreed to release six minors, once they had the agreement in writing. They argued that the deceased teacher could wait since the priority was to preserve the lives of the captives. So the criminals asked Moisés to return to the kindergarten with a physician and a cameraman, the latter who had been filming the scene from the perimeters of the security fence.

Soon the two volunteers were ready to accompany Moisés into the building. Once inside, the head criminal demanded that the doctor examine each of the children, including themselves. The doctor immediately began examining all the children. While this was happening, he ordered the cameraman to film each of them to show that they were alive and unharmed. The reason the ringleader also had his own state of health filmed was a precaution in order to prevent a possible attack by the police, known for torturing and abusing detainees. Once Moisés obtained the video, he and the two volunteers asked six children to come with them to be released. The two volunteers took the children into their arms and quickly left the building. Moisés, with two children in his arms would be the last to leave the building. Once he was outside, the public crowded around the security fence and began to clap. The crowd was moved by his courage. After handing the children over to the police Commissioner, he began to speak to the Judge and prosecutor in order to secure the agreement. Fifteen minutes after signing the agreement, the three firsts villains surrendered with his hands up, and his gun hanging from his index finger. Three of the children came out with them and one adult. Half an hour later, a fourth criminal emerged from the building followed by the criminal lead and the rest of the hostages.

The authorities were certain that they were dealing with dangerous criminals. They were sure that despite their agreement, the bandits would be given a long prison sentence due to their criminal record.

However, when the Prosecutor verified their signatures and fingerprints, they were met with a surprise. Their criminal records were as clear as water. None of them even had received a traffic infringement. The prosecutor realized that these bandits were first time offenders. However, the prosecutor remained optimistic; she was sure that the weight of the law would bear down on the criminal band for murder. However, when the police looked for the teacher's corpse in the bathroom, they surprisingly found her alive and his body completely intact.

With this new piece of knowledge the prosecutor no longer had a strong case since she could not accuse them of a crime that did not exist. The only possible evidence she had to build her case were some videos of robberies. She hoped to prove that these criminals were the same ones that appeared in the videos. However, although her logic was sound, she soon realized that her efforts would be futile. While comparing the projected images, no clear characteristics appeared to show that they were the same band of criminals; rather, the videos demonstrated that the criminals operated in an entirely different way. The same thing happened with the use of weapons and the physical appearance of the jewelry thieves. Due to these discrepancies, the prosecutor concluded that she must be wrong and it wasn't in fact the same criminal band. The only way the authorities could punish them with the full weight of the law would be if the bandits admitted their guilt to previous assaults. However, this would not be advisable for them and they continued to deny previous criminal activity. So during the eventual trial, the judge only found them guilty of illegal possession of weapons and they were sentenced to five years in prison. Because they studied and worked diligently while in prison, they were set free after only thirty-two months.

Moisés admitted to me that by omitting the fact that the teacher had not been killed, he had betrayed the authorities. However, the primary objective had been achieved: the freedom and safety of all the hostages along with the peaceful surrendering of the bandits to police.

Years Later

The following three years flew by. Moisés continued to be invited to lecture in various towns and cities and as his assistant, I accompanied him on every trip and to every event. One day, we arrived at an event in a school located in the south part of the capital. After parking the car we both began walking towards to the University, where the conference would be held. But a few steps before arriving at our destination, several men wearing elegant suits, blocked our path. "Moisés, Moisés", they called out waving to him. Suddenly Moisés realized who they were and his mouth dropped open in surprise. They were the criminal band that had held the hostages in the Kindergarten a few years ago. They approached us and then each one of them hugged Moisés and thanked him for intervening during the conflict, which proved to be a critical juncture in each of their lives.

After I introduced myself and we greeted each other, they told us that four months ago they had been released from prison, but their stay in the penitentiary had not been in vain. They had started a Bible study there, they explained. Through God's teachings, they had learned that their efforts to help the poor and needy through robberies and illegal actions could be carried out correctly without putting people's possessions or business's at risk. God they said, had transformed their inner beings and now the violent acts had become part of their past.

Their story was one of the many personal satisfactions Moisés was blessed with. He now understood that he could transform people's lives and help guide them out of misfortune and onto a better path. According to Moisés, if these men now helped others in similar situations as they had been, our world would transform for the better.

Minutes after I finished telling Moisés's story, and realizing that his lecture would soon commence, I glanced over at Moisés, sitting with the President of the company on the far side of the room. Soon he rose from his chair and made his way to the stage to begin his presentation. As soon as he got up and started walking toward the stage, all the board members beside me stood up and began to applaud. The applause spread through the room and like wild fire grew to the sound of a roar.

The end

Author's Overview

I think that many readers will find it incredible and unusual that so many negative events could happen to one person. However, what readers should focus on is how this character faced his misfortune, and managed to recover astoundingly from each devastating experience.

HOME

A true odyssey is a battle between the misfortune and courage. Where the most vulnerable of the two contenders, when had not option come out victorious. By dishonest way the winner achieved to give a setback to his fate. With this unexpected change, he could realize that, "no matter how difficult the problem is, there is always a solution".

Author's Note

This story is based on real life events and people. In order to respect the privacy of these individuals, names and places have been changed. Any resemblance to reality is pure coincidence.

LibrosEnRed Publishing House

LibrosEnRed is the most complete digital publishing house in the Spanish language. Since June 2000 we have published and sold digital and printed-on-demand books. Our mission is to help all authors publish their work and offer the readers fast and economic access to all types of books.

We publish novels, stories, poems, research theses, manuals, and monographs. We cover a wide range of contents. We offer the possibility to commercialize and promote new titles through the Internet to millions of potential readers.

Enter www.librosenred.com to see our catalog, comprising of hundreds of classic titles and contemporary authors.

CPSIA information can be obtained at www.ICGtesting.com
Printed in the USA
LVOW07s0104041214

416997LV00001B/4/P